TO THE DEATH

When Nathan Palmer and Jeff Morgan take up bare-knuckle boxing, they soon regret their decision: the result of the fight has been decided beforehand, and they find themselves running from the aggrieved sheriff and townsfolk of Lone Gulch. They seek to make amends, but that leads to taking part in another fight — one where the stakes will be as high as they can get. Unbeknown to the two pards, they have become embroiled in a secret world where rich men pay to watch boxers fight to the death . . .

SCOTT CONNOR

TO THE DEATH

Complete and Unabridged

LINFORD
Leicester

First published in Great Britain in 2017 by
Robert Hale
an imprint of The Crowood Press
Wiltshire

First Linford Edition
published 2019
by arrangement with
The Crowood Press
Wiltshire

A catalogue record for this book is available
from the British Library.

ISBN 978–1–4448–4303–3

Published by
F. A. Thorpe (Publishing)
Anstey, Leicestershire

Set by Words & Graphics Ltd.
Anstey, Leicestershire
Printed and bound in Great Britain by
T. J. International Ltd., Padstow, Cornwall

This book is printed on acid-free paper

1

'Fifty dollars on the big man!'

Nathan Palmer hadn't expected that anyone would wager such a large bet; he cast a worried glance at Jeff Morgan.

'Don't worry,' Jeff said, leaning towards him. 'This can still work out.'

'But that means two hundred dollars have been staked on Harris,' Nathan said. He looked at Jeff's opponent across the square that had been marked out in the barn. 'Only five dollars have been staked on you. And I bet that!'

Jeff laughed, but when the latest bet encouraged a flurry of punters to gamble, he looked just as worried as Nathan. The offered odds on Harris Twain were five dollars returned for every four dollars staked, as opposed to twenty dollars returned for every dollar staked if Jeff won.

These odds weren't unexpected. Jeff

was a large man, but Harris was a head taller than he was, his arms were thicker than Jeff's legs, and his bony, angular face looked as if it had withstood many a pummelling.

When the hubbub had died down the bookmaker, Maddox Fincher, gestured for the referee Gene Hansen to enter the ring.

'Our fighters tonight are Harris Twain and Jeff Morgan,' Gene called.

Nathan removed Jeff's long jacket, leaving him bare-chested.

Harris, on the other hand, shrugged his own jacket from his shoulders and let it fall to the ground to expose his barrel-like chest. Then he stood with his large fists raised to head height, showing off biceps that bulged like small, misshapen bags of corn.

'The bigger they are . . . ' Nathan said, slapping Jeff on the back.

' . . . the harder they hit,' Jeff finished with a gulp. He moved off. He chose a spot a third of the way into the ring; his opponent stayed on the edge of the ring.

Around fifty men and a handful of women had congregated in secret at sundown in an abandoned homestead ten miles out of Lone Gulch to watch what had been billed as a young hopeful taking on a seasoned veteran.

Gene paraded around the marked-out area. He directed the audience to stand at least ten feet away, only the seconds being allowed to stand beside their respective corners.

Even when everyone was in position Gene continued fussing, presenting the air of a man who enjoyed being in charge, even though the contest was illegal.

'Fifty dollars to the winner, only bruises to the loser,' Gene proclaimed when he'd deemed that the arrangements were to his satisfaction. 'London Prize-ring rules will apply.'

His statement made Harris smile for the first time, revealing a mouth that had more gaps than teeth, and Nathan couldn't help but smile too. He had been given a list of the rules. So far he had noted five transgressions.

Gene beckoned the two men to approach the scratch in the centre of the ring and shake hands, which each did without meeting the other's eye. Then they moved back to their corners and, with shouts of encouragement ringing out on all sides, the bout got under way.

Jeff raised his fists in front of his face and moved sideways, taking quick nimble steps, while Harris stomped three long paces forward to claim the centre of the ring. There he waited for Jeff to make the first move; he didn't even raise his fists.

Jeff paced around all four corners, making Harris turn to watch his progress. Jeff's apparent agility encouraged several people to bet on him, but the others shouted at him to make a move.

Nathan caught his eye and raised crossed fingers. Jeff smiled. Then he darted in, delivered a short-armed jab into Harris's stomach, then swayed back.

When Harris folded over the blow, gasping out a long breath, Jeff rocked forward on to his toes. Then he bunched his fist as he moved in to repeat the blow. That proved to be an unwise move, for Harris recovered quickly and, with a contemptuous shove to Jeff's shoulders, bundled him away.

Jeff stepped backwards rapidly, but he failed to keep his balance. He tipped over, landing on his back. Quickly he raised himself to a sitting position, snarling in irritation at having been knocked down so easily.

As the fall concluded the round Nathan hurried over to give Jeff water.

'I've only been fighting for a minute,' Jeff said when Nathan knelt beside him. 'I don't need a drink yet.'

'Drink it anyhow,' Nathan said. 'Take every chance for a rest you can.'

Jeff did as he was told and took the maximum amount of time before the second round started. Thirty seconds later he got another break, although that was only because he'd been bundled to the ground again by the force of an even firmer shove.

'I'm not resting this time,' Jeff said,

directing Nathan to stay in his corner with a wave. Then he leapt to his feet.

Fifteen seconds later he was lying on his back again; a groan was the only sound he could utter. Harris had landed his first punch, a round-armed blow to the chin that had lifted Jeff bodily off the ground so that he slammed down heavily five feet away.

Nathan raised Jeff's shoulders to make him sit up. Then he tried to make him drink.

Jeff merely sat slumped over, unable even to hold his head up. Nathan poured the water over his head, to which Jeff made his first reaction by pushing the bottle away.

'Nobody's placing bets any more,' Nathan said, speaking in Jeff's ear so as to be heard beneath the hubbub of derision for Jeff and encouragement for Harris that was sounding on all sides.

'I'm doing that well, am I?' Jeff said, rubbing his chin ruefully.

'You sure are.' Nathan lowered his

voice to a whisper. 'Everything's going according to plan.'

Heartened, Jeff jumped to his feet, ran on the spot and shook his upper body vigorously. Then he faced up to Harris, who regarded him with a sorrowful shaking of his head.

Harris glanced at his second, Keenan, who gave him a quick nod. Then, in slow and confident paces, he moved towards Jeff.

This time Jeff stood his ground and when Harris threw a high punch at his head he ducked beneath it. Then he rose up and danced forward, using his momentum to give extra force to his swinging punch.

The blow landed squarely on Harris's ear with a heavy crunch that made Jeff wring his bruised hand while Harris screeched and doubled over. The shouting from the audience drowned out his groans as Harris clutched his head, trying to dull the pain.

Then Harris toppled over like a felled tree. He slammed down in the dirt on his side, sending up a billowing cloud of dust.

Several seconds passed before Gene got over his surprise to declare the fourth round had ended. Several more seconds passed before Keenan shook off his apparent shock and went to kneel beside Harris.

'And the harder they fall,' Nathan said when Jeff joined him in his corner.

Jeff ignored his cheerful attitude as he prodded worriedly over his bruised hand. Nathan reckoned that Jeff had inadvertently happened upon the most sensible way to behave and he took his time in filling Jeff's water bottle, being careful not to catch anyone's eye.

Around the ring the cries of surprise turned to grunts of anger. When Nathan looked up Harris was still lying where he'd fallen, while Keenan was fussing over him.

Keenan tipped a bucket of water over Harris's head, but that only made him stir weakly and groan, then roll over to lie on his back.

Though Gene had no option but to declare Jeff the winner he walked back and forth across the ring several times, watching while Keenan slapped Harris's cheeks, giving him every chance to get back on his feet.

The delay only allowed time for the audience's grumbling discontent to grow as the suspicion spread that something was wrong. The gradual change in the mood made Jeff pay attention to proceedings.

'Gene will declare me the winner, won't he?' he asked.

'That's what Maddox Fincher said he'd have to do, but that'll be only half the battle.' Nathan cast a glance at the audience, most of whom were now glaring at them. 'We then have to get out of here alive.'

Both men rose to their feet to await the verdict, but before Gene could speak up a gunshot sounded, coming from the back of the audience. Nathan had expected trouble, but he hadn't expected it to start this quickly — or for it to be so decisive.

The noise even made Harris sit up straight, adding further credence to the possibility that the fight hadn't been conducted fairly.

Luckily nobody noticed this suggestion of his recovery as everyone turned to face the three men who had sneaked into the barn. These men were now blocking the doorway.

'I'm Sheriff Armstrong Beck,' one of them said. He stepped forward with his gun raised high. 'These are my deputies Livingston Beck and Emerson Tate. Your evening's entertainment is over.'

For several seconds there was total silence as everyone in the barn glanced at each other. Then one man ran for the door and that started a stampede.

There was a general rush for the door. The lawmen stepped aside to let the people pass, although they eyed each individual with keen interest.

After the first wave of people had fled the lawmen stopped some men. Armstrong murmured a quick question, which was answered with shrugs or non-committal replies, after which he let the men pass.

Nathan got the impression they were stopping men they didn't recognize while noting who had been here so that they could deal with everyone later in a less fraught situation.

As they were new to the area Nathan reckoned that mingling with the crowd was their best option.

He found Jeff's jacket and helped him into it. Then, adopting the same posture as everyone else by keeping their heads down, the two men joined the hurrying crowd.

With all thoughts of reprisals amongst the erst-while audience gone, they merged in easily until Emerson's heavy hand slapped down on Nathan's shoulder. He dragged him sideways to stand before the sheriff. A moment later Livingston repeated the operation with Jeff.

'Where's Vencer Muerte?' Armstrong asked.

Nathan shrugged. 'I've never heard of him.'

Armstrong narrowed his eyes with distrust. Then Emerson leaned towards him.

'That man was fighting,' he said, indicating Jeff. 'The other man was the second.'

Armstrong gestured for the pair to stand at one side of the barn. Then he returned to examining the rest of the crowd, which had thinned out to a steady trickle.

His gaze had yet to fall on Harris, Keenan and Maddox, the other men who had been involved in rigging the fight, but these men had noticed that the deputies had waylaid Nathan and Jeff. So they had bunched up and were talking briefly.

It seemed that their deliberations had reached a conclusion when they made a run for the door.

Their sudden movement caught Armstrong's eye. He glanced at Livingston, who moved in quickly. While Emerson guarded Nathan and Jeff, Livingston stood in the way of Keenan and Harris.

Armstrong was left to block Maddox's escape route.

Harris and Keenan darted to the left and right, but when Livingston followed their movements and spread his arms they thought better of trying to barge past him and slowed to a halt. Maddox, though, ran on with his head down.

Armstrong raised an imperious hand. Maddox swerved around him, forcing Armstrong to make a grab for him. The sheriff grabbed a fleeting hold of his jacket before Maddox tore free and slipped out through the door.

Maddox then struggled to find a way through the dispersing people who were trying to reach their horses. He settled for turning on his heel and running along the side of the barn. That route took him towards the advancing sheriff. Maddox skidded to a halt and the two men looked each other in the eye for the first time.

Through the doorway Nathan saw Maddox offer a thin smile, at which

Armstrong jerked upright and backed away for a pace, seemingly surprised. Then Maddox ran at him, bundled him aside and fled, disappearing from view.

Armstrong landed on his side in a patch of muddy ground, where he was struggling to get back up. Inside the barn the deputies shot worried glances at each other. Then Emerson left to help Armstrong get back on his feet, leaving Livingston guarding Harris and Keenan.

Jeff looked at Nathan and winked.

'Nobody's watching us no more,' he said, his voice low.

'I know, but we got arrested,' Nathan said.

Jeff shrugged. 'If we were important they'd have guarded us better.'

Nathan weighed up the situation; it seemed that nobody was paying them any attention. A smile spread over his face and he slapped Jeff on the back.

Then they ran for the door.

2

'Those two aren't saying nothing,' Deputy Emerson Tate said as he left the jailhouse that adjoined the law office.

Sheriff Armstrong Beck went to the stove and hunched over it to let the heat dry his muddy clothing. When it became clear that he wouldn't respond his son, Deputy Livingston Beck, spoke up.

'Harris is a fighter, and despite his size he's not a good one,' he said. 'So I doubt he or his second will tell us who organized the fight, whether there'll be another one, and whether Vencer Muerte was ever supposed to be there.'

'Perhaps Vencer was never going to show,' Emerson said with a sigh.

Armstrong shook his head. 'Most of the details Oscar McClellan gave me about the fight were correct.'

'As Oscar himself attended the fight,

that surely proves it was just local people enjoying some good-natured boxing,' Emerson opined. 'Perhaps if Lone Gulch's townsfolk choose to watch men pummel each other instead of getting into fights themselves, we should let them.'

Armstrong clenched his hands into fists and then turned to Emerson.

'Oscar always tells me anything he finds out about bare-knuckle fights, and as fights are against the law, we were right to uphold the law. Tonight I wanted to make more arrests, but most of the people were only spectators and I couldn't arrest half the town.'

Emerson smiled. 'Since I first met you, your attitude has softened. Once you *would* have arrested half the town.'

Armstrong took the opportunity to lighten up; he smiled briefly. 'If it happens again I won't be so lenient. But I'm sorry I failed you by letting Maddox Fincher get away.'

'You knew that man?' Livingston said.

'I met him once, briefly. It was a long time ago and that only goes to confirm I'm getting too old for this work.'

Emerson and Livingston were used to him grumbling about the number of years he'd served Lone Gulch, so they both relaxed. Emerson sat at his desk while Livingston fetched a coffee pot and moved to the stove, but Armstrong stepped to the side to block his way.

'What's wrong?' Livingston asked.

'For you, nothing,' Armstrong replied with a warm smile. 'Tomorrow, I'm handing in my star. Lone Gulch needs a competent sheriff. If I go now, I'll know the town will be in good hands.'

Livingston opened and closed his mouth soundlessly, then he shook off his surprise by gesturing at Emerson to busy himself elsewhere. Armstrong raised a hand, bidding him to stay.

'You can't retire now,' Livingston said when he eventually found his voice.

Armstrong smiled and glanced down at his muddied knees.

'I knew the time would come, but I

didn't know when. As it turned out, my day came when I lay in a puddle outside Oscar McClellan's old house having found that the man I came to arrest wasn't there and the man I'd tried to arrest was running away.'

'It'd been raining. Any one of us could have been knocked over on the slippery ground. There's no reason to be so annoyed that you give up.'

'There's every reason. Tonight Maddox did me a service and if I ignore the warning, the next time I could get a bullet in the guts from some trigger-happy kid.'

'But what will you do instead?'

Armstrong rocked his head from side to side before he replied:

'Perhaps I'll find Maddox and thank him.'

★　★　★

'I reckon we've finally thrown Gene Hansen off,' Jeff said. He bent over and placed his hands on his knees as he

18

gathered his breath.

Nathan leaned back against the saloon wall and stood tall; he too was breathing deeply. In the distance shouting sounded as Gene Hansen and the aggrieved crowd from the fight tried to work out where the pair had gone.

'After we've ruined his fight, Gene will never give up,' he said between gasps. 'We should never have come to Lone Gulch.'

Jeff stood up straight and set off down the board-walk.

'If we're going to talk about the things we should never have done, we can start with the day we met Harris and Keenan.'

When they reached the corner of the next building Nathan muttered that he agreed. Then he glanced over his shoulder.

Four buildings back a group of people led by Gene Hansen were spilling out on to the main drag, shaking their fists and glaring around angrily.

Nathan tried to get Jeff's attention

with a worried grunt, but then he walked into his back. The two men went sprawling against the wall before Nathan saw what had worried Jeff.

Ahead, another group of men, led by Oscar McClellan, was pacing out into the main drag and looking around, presumably for them.

'Trapped,' Nathan murmured unhappily; he became even more disgruntled when Oscar pointed at them. Then the group broke into a run.

In response, Nathan and Jeff turned on their heels, but when Oscar hollered down the main drag Gene saw them. Quickly Gene beckoned his group to start running too.

Nathan would have run past the saloon doorway, but Jeff's hand slapped down on his shoulder and turned him towards the saloon. That refuge seemed as though it might leave them even more trapped, but one look at the mobs closing in from two directions convinced him that they didn't have a choice.

He followed Jeff as he ducked into

the saloon. It turned out to be a quiet establishment with only a dozen customers sitting at tables or standing at the bar. Nobody looked at them.

Nathan searched for an exit. He found that only one other door led out of the room and it was behind the bar. He pointed at it, but Jeff's gaze had rested on one of the men standing at the bar: Deputy Emerson Tate.

Nathan winced. With a jerk of his head he directed Jeff to head back outside before the lawman saw them; then, turning, he saw through the door and the window that people were closing in on the saloon, cutting off all escape routes.

Without a choice they both faced the bar. Then, walking as calmly as possible in the circumstances and avoiding catching anyone's eye, they moved on.

The racket outside made the customers crane their necks and peer through the windows. Then the first wave of fist-shaking pursuers burst in.

'You two are going to get the beating

you should have got earlier,' Gene shouted.

Nathan and Jeff exchanged worried glances. They broke into a run then skidded to a halt when Emerson stepped sideways and blocked their path.

'You're wrong, Gene,' Emerson declared. He looked over Nathan's shoulder at the men who were pouring into the saloon. 'Nobody gets beaten tonight.'

'They cheated these people out of their money,' Gene said, gesturing angrily. 'They can't get away with that.'

Emerson set his feet wide apart and faced the pursuers as they jockeyed for positions and shouted out demands. He said nothing, exuding quiet authority, as he waited for everyone to calm down.

Even when the mob had quietened, he did nothing other than smile for almost a minute; the delay made everyone shuffle and cast concerned glances at each other.

Nathan was still catching his breath after the chase. It took him a while to realize why the situation had amused the deputy. When he looked at Jeff he was nodding, as if he'd only just understood the irony of the confrontation, too.

Oscar McClellan appeared to pick up on the problem first by sloping away, but Emerson didn't wait for everyone to understand. He walked up to Gene.

'Tonight an illegal fight took place. Anybody who attended it broke the law.' Emerson paced back and forth twice along the front row of a crowd in which everyone was now standing stiffly. 'So, would you like to explain your complaint again, Gene?'

'The mayor doesn't reckon we did anything wrong tonight. After all, you can't arrest half the town.'

'I can't, but I could arrest one man.'

Gene met Emerson's eye and managed a thin smile that acknowledged his predicament.

'I have no complaint,' he said through gritted teeth.

Emerson nodded and moved along the front row. Nobody met his eye and nobody else spoke up.

'In that case,' he declared, 'I'd be obliged if you'd leave me to enjoy my drink in peace.'

Even before he'd finished speaking several men in the back row turned away and scurried outside. Seeing their numbers dwindling, the rest backed down without complaint but, finding the doorway blocked, Gene dallied to cast an angry glare at Nathan and Jeff that promised them that despite this setback the matter wasn't over.

Emerson maintained his smile until the last of the mob had left. Then he turned to Nathan and Jeff.

'Obliged,' Nathan said.

Emerson nodded and beckoned them to join him at the bar. Again, he didn't speak for a while as he presumably waited for the remaining customers to lose interest. Even then he spoke quietly.

'Do you want to explain what happened?' he asked.

Nathan took a deep breath.

'We *did* take part in that fight,' he

said. 'I was the second and Jeff was the fighter.'

Emerson cast a glance at Jeff, noting his large hands and a physique that looked bulky now that he wasn't standing next to the even larger Harris Twain.

'I guess you look like a fighter.'

'I might look like one, but I'm not,' Jeff said with a sigh. 'The result had been decided beforehand.'

'Obliged for the truth.' Emerson rubbed his jaw as he pondered. 'But I'd guess you admitted that only because you hope I'll arrest you and that by the time you come out of jail Gene will have forgotten about you.'

Nathan coughed with embarrassment as Emerson astutely picked up on the reason for their honesty.

'It's the safest option,' Nathan said. 'Last month we went to a fight where Harris Twain was beaten by a man who was half his size, which didn't concern us as we'd played the odds. We won fifty dollars, but the crowd rebelled and we

25

never collected our money.'

'The winner barely escaped with his life, while we chased after Harris and Keenan,' Jeff said, picking up the story. 'When we caught up with them they admitted they'd been following Maddox's instructions to fix the fight, but they'd failed to convince the audience because their ringer was too puny to make his victory believable.'

Nathan and Jeff shot embarrassed glances at each other, leaving Emerson to complete the story.

'They sold you the idea of taking over the ringer role,' he said.

'Yeah,' Jeff said. 'Tonight was my first fight. After what happened, it'll be my last.'

'And what happened to the other men involved in this ruse?'

'We thought you'd arrested Harris and Keenan while Maddox got away.'

'With everyone's money,' Nathan added.

'That sums up the situation,' Emerson said. He downed his whiskey. 'And that means you can join Harris and Keenan in jail. Maddox will join you soon.'

Emerson gestured to them to walk ahead of him. They didn't object. When they reached the board-walk they found that their pursuers had melted into town.

One crisis had been averted but Nathan was now worried that the legal punishment for their activities might be worse than whatever Gene had intended to do to them.

'How can we make this right, like Gene did?' he wondered as they walked along.

'You can't.'

'But we didn't organize anything. We just did what Maddox told us to do.'

Emerson didn't reply until they reached the law office where he stopped by the door.

'So where is Vencer Muerte?'

'We've never heard of him.'

'Where is Maddox Fincher?'

'We don't know. We really don't know nothing.'

Emerson shrugged. 'Then I have no choice.'

Emerson pushed them on towards the door, but Nathan dug in a heel and swung round.

'Wait,' he said. Nathan waved his arms as he struggled to recall a detail about Maddox that might help them, but Jeff spoke up.

'We know nothing about Maddox,' he said, 'but we discussed tonight's arrangements at this trading post twenty miles outside town.'

Emerson brightened and nodded.

'Obliged,' he said. 'That might give the law somewhere to start.'

Nathan and Jeff both sighed with relief. Emerson opened the door and pushed them through.

'Hey, we were helpful,' Nathan said.

'You were,' Emerson said, 'but the problem is Sheriff Beck doesn't let his deputies do deals with outlaws. You two are still under arrest.'

3

'I'm pleased my son will be looking after Lone Gulch,' Armstrong said. This declaration caused a sharp intake of breath from both Emerson and Livingston.

'So you're really leaving?' Livingston said, his jaw jutting. 'I'd hoped you'd reconsider overnight.'

'I didn't. You're ready for this and you have a capable deputy. Mayor Garrett will see you at noon to deal with the formalities. Then you'll have three months until the next elections to prove you're the right man for the appointment.'

'If I'm the right man it's only because of you.' Livingston smiled. 'And I hope I can still call on your advice.'

'You can't.' Armstrong frowned. 'I'm leaving town for a while, perhaps a month, perhaps more. It'll let you make the job your own, and there are a few things I've always wanted to do.'

'I guess I'm obliged,' Livingston said, although his low tone suggested otherwise. 'What have you always wanted to do?'

Armstrong smiled, the expression at odds with his tense demeanour.

'I'll tell you when I get back.'

Armstrong turned to the door, but Livingston stepped sideways and blocked his way.

'Have you any last orders, sir?'

Armstrong set his hands on his hips and thought for a bit. Then he waved a dismissive hand at the jail-house.

'Warn your prisoners and then release them at sundown. A night in a cell should have dampened their enthusiasm for fighting; if that doesn't work, the people who lost money will find a means to do it.'

Livingston smiled. 'I'll do that. And thank you, for everything.'

Armstrong coughed several times to clear his tight throat, then he shook his son's hand.

Emerson came over and took his hand. They stood in an awkward silence until Armstrong opened the door.

He took a pace forward. Then he stopped, turned and looked around the office, knowing this was the last time he'd do this as an official.

When he had finished his survey of what had been his domain he was facing Livingston. With a smile he moved forward and clamped both hands on his son's shoulders.

'Uphold the law at all times and in all situations, son,' he said, his voice gruff with emotion for the first time. 'Then every problem you'll ever face will resolve itself.'

'I know,' Livingston said, his voice also catching. 'I'll follow your lead.'

Armstrong shook his head. 'Don't. I learnt that lesson the hard way. You don't need to.'

Livingston furrowed his brow, but before he could ask his father to explain his cryptic comment, Armstrong had turned smartly away.

★ ★ ★

'What are your first orders, Sheriff?' asked Emerson, breaking the contemplative silence.

Thirty minutes had passed since Armstrong left town, so Livingston took the opportunity to lighten his pensive mood with a smile.

'While I give the prisoners that warning, see how people are reacting to my father's news,' he said.

'Understood.' Emerson got up to go but he stopped beside Livingston's desk. He lowered his voice. 'I'm sorry the raid last night didn't work out the way we hoped, in all ways.'

'It's not your fault my father retired. So listen out for news of more fights. If you hear anyone talking about Vencer Muerte, tell me. Even if we follow another nine leads that turn out to be blind I won't hesitate to follow a tenth.'

Emerson nodded and left the office. For the next hour he did as requested and patrolled around town, talking with people and listening to chatter when it turned to the recent news.

Nobody was surprised that Sheriff Armstrong Beck had retired, although everyone was surprised he'd left town so abruptly. On the other hand, everybody accepted that his actions were typical of the man's unassuming nature; they thought his son would carry on his good work.

Emerson was returning to the law office when his steadily paced patrol took him past Yardley Weston's hardware store. The old rotting store sign that usually stood propped up against the wall was lying face down on the boardwalk again.

Emerson winced and came to a sudden halt, not having expected to see this. For the last week the sign's being tipped over had been the secret — and unwelcome — signal that he had new instructions.

His heart thudding, Emerson righted the sign. Then he plodded to the stables and round to the back, where he stood leaning against the wall.

For twenty minutes he stood casting his gaze over the plains. The wait only made him brood. So when the back door creaked open for a few inches it took all his willpower not to turn towards it.

'Last night went badly,' the familiar voice said in a low monotone. 'After that farce of a bout, a special second fight was to have been staged for a select few, except your sheriff made sure that didn't happen. Dangerous people are angry.'

Emerson took several deep breaths before he replied:

'You didn't tell me about the second bout, and you failed to keep the fight secret. Armstrong heard a rumour about it, and as he wanted to catch Vencer Muerte I couldn't stop him . . . ' Emerson trailed off. His voice had sounded nervous even to his own ears and he accepted that weak excuses wouldn't help him now.

'Don't blame others. Keeping Armstrong away from the fight was your only task, and you failed.'

'It's impossible to keep a diligent lawman from doing his duty.' Emerson shrugged. 'But Armstrong handed in his star this morning and his son isn't as headstrong.'

A throaty chuckle sounded. 'I'd heard, and that means last night wasn't a complete disaster.'

The man had spoken quickly and this time the voice was a little more lively. Emerson had always assumed that his tormentor used a flat tone to disguise his voice; now he resolved to pay attention in future in case he again slipped up.

'So there will be another special fight?'

'Sure, two days from now at sundown.'

'Where?'

'As you couldn't keep Armstrong away from a fight when you knew where it'd be held, I'm not telling you where this one will be.'

'Then don't blame me if things go wrong again.'

'I shall.' The man sighed. 'Either way, just keep to your original instructions, but this time make sure the new sheriff is busy elsewhere at the right time.'

Emerson nodded. 'Will those dangerous people be there?'

A sharp intake of breath sounded. 'You're asking too many questions. Last night you failed. From now on no more mistakes or you know what'll happen.'

Emerson waited for more instructions, but when they didn't come he edged closer to the door.

'Except, if I do this I never want to hear from you again. I'm not the man I used to be and I've forged a decent life here. Even if it destroys me I won't try to stop my fellow lawmen from doing their duty again.'

Having delivered the speech he'd been gathering the courage to make for the past week, Emerson waited, but he heard only silence. He turned to the door; to his irritation his tormentor had gone.

4

Five horses were in the corral beside the trading post. Armstrong Beck dismounted quickly and paced around the building.

He ducked beneath the windows as he entered through the only door, at the front of the building; an apparently cautious tactic that was sure to attract more attention than if he'd just marched straight in.

Three men were sitting at a table sharing a jug of beer. They avoided looking at him with a studied lack of interest.

Armstrong waited until the owner, Quentin Saunders, came up to the counter before he closed the door behind him. Quentin trod a careful path between helping people who were on the wrong side of the law while also giving the law information, provided that neither of these services endangered himself.

Armstrong hoped that news of his retirement hadn't reached him yet, as he knew which side of the path Quentin would tread today. He got his answer when Quentin gave him a cheery smile.

'I heard about last night's fight,' he called. 'Everyone was having fun. Then you arrived.'

The more animated Quentin was, the more information he would provide; this statement meant that someone who had been involved with the fight had been here.

'The people who are now in a jail cell aren't having fun,' Armstrong said.

'How many?'

'Four arrested so far. That'll be doubled before sundown.'

'Four more arrests and yet those people were just enjoying a few hours of entertainment.' Quentin scowled. 'You're not completing your work here, lawman.'

The three men at the table grunted supportive comments, but Armstrong ignored them, noting that in his usual subtle way Quentin had confirmed that a fourth, unseen person was here. Armstrong couldn't risk asking more questions; he headed over to the table.

'You men know Maddox Fincher?'

The three men made a show of looking confused, but none of them replied, so giving Armstrong all the information he needed. He moved on towards the bar.

While he waited for Maddox to accidentally betray his presence he leaned on the counter and thought about his reason for undertaking this private mission: a reason that harked back four years to his first month as a lawman.

★ ★ ★

Back then, twenty years of military service culminating in his achieving the rank of major had filled him with confidence. But the reality of his new job had turned out to be tougher than he'd expected.

39

Dealing with undisciplined non-military people was messy and, although he wouldn't admit it, for his first few weeks he'd struggled.

His first serious case had tested his resolve to breaking point. Rumours of an illegal boxing match sent him on several false trails until he arrived in Hickory Point.

The fight was already over. People were fleeing from a stable. Only three people didn't escape him and they hadn't tried.

One fighter had been beaten to a pulp. His opponent, a local man, Grant McClellan, was dying.

The third man was Maddox Fincher. Dollar bills filled Maddox's pockets, courtesy of the bets he'd taken, but he'd stayed to help the injured boxers.

Maddox couldn't help Grant so Armstrong had knelt beside the dying boxer and asked him for details.

In reply, Grant had whispered, 'Vencer Muerte.'

He didn't speak again, neither for

that matter did anyone else. Armstrong arrested Maddox and the winning boxer, Wardell Evans, but neither of them would talk about the night's events and neither man would explain who Vencer Muerte was.

The next few weeks were frustrating.

He had been used to dispensing swift military justice to men of honour who would often admit to their crimes. He wasn't used to men who wouldn't talk and a legal process that required evidence and statements.

He could find no witnesses who would speak up, so the evidence he gathered wasn't strong enough to charge Wardell with killing Grant, either accidentally or deliberately.

All he could charge Wardell and Maddox with was the minor misdemeanour of taking part in an illegal boxing match.

He had to decide whether to press on with trying to prove they were guilty of more serious crimes or let them go. In the end, reluctantly, he had released Maddox.

Then he'd followed him in the hope that he'd lead him to someone, but Maddox left the county without dallying to speak with anyone.

Armstrong tried the same plan with Wardell, this time staying further away in the hope that he'd lull him into a false sense of security. But when he caught up with Wardell the man had been shot in the back.

Again, nobody had seen anything and nobody knew why Wardell had been killed.

Oscar McClellan hadn't viewed this conclusion as being justice for his son, although his failure to be cheered by Wardell's death convinced Armstrong that he hadn't killed him.

Wardell's wife Ruth had been even angrier. She rode into town and demanded to know why the sheriff hadn't stopped her husband from being killed.

His explanation that the situation had been complicated hadn't sounded convincing even to his own ears and she had gone away unsatisfied.

These incidents having come to an unacceptable conclusion, he resolved to do better, and in the following years he served Lone Gulch with distinction.

Four years passed without any developments until Oscar McClellan told him that an illegal boxing match was to be staged at the homestead he'd abandoned when he moved into town. McClellan had also heard that Vencer Muerte would attend. Armstrong vowed that this time he'd get answers.

★   ★   ★

A rustling sounded, breaking into Armstrong's ruminations. He reckoned someone was trying to sneak away quietly so he moved away from the counter.

With a heavy tread he walked to the first row of the piled-up goods that filled half the room. He prodded a corn sack with the toe of his boot while watching the table.

The two men who had their backs to him were hunched over the table, but the third man couldn't stop himself from watching Armstrong move along the row of supplies.

Armstrong stopped by each pile, but he didn't look over to the men, preferring to let Maddox reveal himself.

He reached the end of a row and was moving to slip into the first aisle when the watching man flicked his gaze to one side, then tried to mask the movement by lowering his head.

That warning put Armstrong on alert just a moment before a creak sounded and the endmost pile of sacks toppled towards him.

Armstrong jerked backwards, letting the pile slap into the wall instead of landing on him, while Maddox used a pole with which he'd knocked over the sacks, to vault over the supplies.

Maddox ran for the door but Armstrong waited until the sacks had settled. Then, with a glare directed at the other three men warning them to stay out of this, he set off in pursuit.

He reached the door four paces behind Maddox, who slammed the door behind him as he slipped through. The door didn't catch and it swung open again as Armstrong reached it, letting him step outside without breaking his stride.

Then he had to duck below the pole as Maddox swung it at his head. The pole rebounded off the wall with a clatter as Armstrong sidestepped away, narrowly avoiding a second blow as the pole whistled by a few inches from his chest.

Then he faced Maddox, who gathered a firmer grip of the pole with two hands as he moved towards him.

'Four years was a long time to wait for this,' Maddox said, 'but it'll be worth it when I pound you into the ground.'

Armstrong continued to back away along the wall. When he reached the corner he moved to duck around the side, but Maddox aimed a wild swiping

45

blow at his stomach.

Armstrong couldn't avoid the pole and he didn't try to. Instead, he leapt forward, his forward motion lessening the impact of the wood slamming into his side.

A moment later he was upon Maddox, grabbing his shoulders and driving him backwards.

Maddox tried to fend him off with the pole but, as the two men were pressed together tightly, the wood was more of a hindrance than a help. Then Maddox's feet became tangled up in the pole and he tripped, landing on his back.

Armstrong followed him down, but not before Maddox had spread both hands along the pole. He locked his elbows to keep the pole elevated. Armstrong also put two hands to the pole and pressed down.

For a dozen heartbeats the two men strained, Armstrong forcing his weight down and Maddox using his leverage against the ground to keep Armstrong from getting too close to him.

The impasse couldn't last for ever. Armstrong, with the force of gravity on his side, was not exerting himself as much as Maddox was. Sweat broke out on Maddox's brow. Then his left arm gave way, causing Armstrong to topple forward on to his chest.

Armstrong came to rest still clutching the pole, which was lying across Maddox's neck; the man's arms were splayed out on the ground.

'Seems you can't avoid a crushed neck this time,' Armstrong grunted. He settled the pole into a position where he could close Maddox's windpipe with a quick movement.

Maddox strained, but when Armstrong pressed down as a warning he slumped in defeat.

'Get off me, lawman,' he said. 'You can't prove nothing I've ever done and you can't make me talk about anything.' He glared defiantly up at Armstrong.

Armstrong smiled. Then he shifted his position to kneel on one end of the pole and hold the other end down with a hand.

'You sure?'

'Yeah. I remember you. You follow the rules. You won't harm me.'

Armstrong treated Maddox to a wider smile.

'You're right. Sheriff Beck would take you back to Lone Gulch. Then he'd question you. If you kept silent he'd leave you alone.'

Armstrong waited until Maddox smirked, then edged the pole down for a few inches. 'But I've got bad news. This morning I retired. Now I'm just Armstrong Beck, and Armstrong can do whatever he wants.'

He drew Maddox's attention to his jacket. Seeing that Maddox had noted the lack of a star, he winked. Then he pressed down on the pole, making Maddox splutter and squirm.

Armstrong maintained the stress for several seconds before he relented and rocked back on his heels.

'Why did you retire?' Maddox said,

his tone incredulous.

'I have unfinished business that I couldn't complete as a lawman.'

'With me?'

'It starts with you and it ends with the man you'll take me to: Vencer Muerte.'

'I'm not doing that.' Maddox pushed the pole, but he couldn't dislodge it. 'The things you can do to me with this stick are like a stroll by the creek compared to what the people who know Vencer would do.'

Armstrong snorted. 'In other words, you don't know where Vencer is. You were a no-account varmint four years ago and you're a nothing now.'

Maddox gazed back at him, his lips clamped shut, confirming that he knew Armstrong was trying to wound his pride so that he could boast about his exploits. Then the corners of his lips turned up in a small smile.

'I can't take you to Vencer Muerte, but I can take you to my boss.'

Armstrong swung the pole away; it

went clattering across the ground. Then he held out a hand to help Maddox get up.

'Do it.'

'I will.' Maddox took the hand and laughed. 'Except afterwards, you won't thank me none.'

5

'What are you going to do now?' Nathan asked. Emerson had closed the law office door and he and the other prisoners were standing on the board-walk.

Harris and Keenan gazed at the door, their mouths open, as if they were still unsure whether the new sheriff had played a joke when he'd freed them at sundown after they'd spent less than a day in a cell.

'We'll never fix a fight again,' Keenan said. Harris grunted his support. 'Everything going wrong once was bad enough, but a second time told us something.'

'Which means we have no choice but to do what we did before,' Harris said. 'We fight honestly.'

Nathan and Jeff snorted a laugh.

'And we have no choice but to do

what we did before,' Nathan said. 'We look for work.'

The four men stood in silence for a while, looking up and down the main drag. Finding that nobody paid them any undue attention they shook hands and wished each other well.

Harris and Keenan headed to the stables through the gathering gloom while Nathan and Jeff moved into the shadows in the alley beside the bank.

'I assume we're waiting to see if they're followed before we decide what we're doing,' Jeff said when the other two men had disappeared from view.

'Sure,' Nathan said. 'They got us into this mess. They can help us get out of it.'

Presently Harris and Keenan led their horses out from the stable. They looked around for signs of anyone showing an interest in them before they mounted up. Then, at a slow pace, they took the shortest route to the edge of town.

Aside from the hubbub coming from

the north side of town, where most of the saloons were, Nathan heard nothing untoward. So, after fifteen minutes during which nobody followed their former colleagues, without comment he and Jeff walked to the stables.

They tried to present the same calm demeanour that Harris and Keenan had shown but, spurred on by the hope that they might avoid the recriminations they'd feared, they were ready to leave in ten minutes. Then they took the same route out of town as the others had.

They were thankful to see nobody as they went on their way. When they reached clear ground only a thin sliver of a moon lit the plains; this was fine by Nathan as the low light level would mask their departure.

He turned to Jeff, meaning to ask him whether they should catch up with the others, but the words died on his lips when Jeff pointed a finger forward, his expression one of open-mouthed concern.

Nathan peered into the gloom. He soon saw what had troubled his friend. A dozen riders had formed themselves into a circle 200 yards ahead.

They were looking inwards and, although the light was too poor for Nathan to see what was interesting them, the faint sounds of a scuffle suggested that the apparent lack of interest in the town had been a feint. It seemed that Harris and Keenan had been followed and rounded up after all.

Nathan and Jeff came to a halt. A few moments later their supposition was proved right when the riders parted and Keenan ran out. He hurried on for a few paces until, with a whoop of delight, one of the mounted men looped a rope down around his shoulders. Then, like a steer, he was dragged back into the circle.

'There's too many of them,' Jeff said unhappily.

'I know,' Nathan said, his tone equally despondent. 'If we try anything, all we'll achieve will be to give them someone else to beat.'

Despite their feeling of helplessness, they didn't turn back to town, both men being reluctant to leave their former partners to their fate.

Ideas for a distraction whirled through Nathan's mind, but before he could come up with a decent plan hoofbeats sounded behind them. Nathan swirled round and saw that they too had been followed.

A line of six riders headed by Gene Hansen was approaching. Although there were fewer men than were dealing with Keenan and Harris, Gene could still ensure they wouldn't get away unscathed.

Nathan pointed to clear space. Then they hurried off, taking a route around Lone Gulch so that they could keep their options open as to whether to head across open land or lose themselves in town.

Nathan didn't look back until they were approaching the main drag.

Gene hadn't tried to catch up with them, but the riders had stayed close enough to keep them in sight. Nathan soon saw the reason for their behaviour when he and Jeff turned into town and found that Oscar McClellan was leading another five riders towards them.

Oscar stopped. He cast glances at the other riders, as though he hadn't expected to trap the quarry so easily. Then he ordered the riders to spread out and block the route ahead. When Nathan looked over his shoulder he saw that their pursuers were also spreading out to cut off all escape routes.

'Punch through the gaps and then keep going?' Jeff asked.

'That might work for a while, but I reckon it'll just get their blood up,' Nathan replied.

'We can't stay. We can't go. What can we do?'

Nathan struggled to answer; they were surrounded and Gene and Oscar had moved in. As the circle tightened he looked beyond the riders, hoping that, as before, someone would put a stop to this confrontation, but the only people he could see were their pursuers.

Worse, he recognized many of them as being from the mob that had tried to capture them last night.

'We look for the third option,' he said. When the riders stopped because they'd closed the circle as tightly as they could, he raised his voice.

'Last night you men lost money, but we don't have it. We came out of that fight with nothing.'

Gene Hansen nudged his horse forward to stand in front of them.

'There never was no fight,' he said, 'unless you're claiming that your friend knocked down a man who was a head taller than he is.'

Nathan reckoned that no answer would satisfy these men but the insult made Jeff grunt with irritation. He leaned forward in the saddle.

'You saw the punch I hammered into Harris's face,' he declared, waving a fist. 'It flattened him.'

'That blow would only knock down a man you'd paid to fall over.' Gene

57

rolled his shoulders and raised a fist. 'But not anyone else.'

As the battle lines were drawn the circle of riders murmured happily. Gene encouraged the direction this confrontation was taking by acknowledging the support with a wide grin.

'Nobody could defeat you all,' Jeff shouted, speaking over the rising noise, 'but in a fair fight I could take on any one of you.'

Jeff glared triumphantly at Gene, seemingly content to have responded with a good taunt before they did their worst; to his surprise his comment made the chatter die down. Oscar cast an amused glance at Gene, implying that Jeff had inadvertently played into their hands.

'That's an interesting challenge,' Gene said, speaking slowly with a big smile on his lips. 'I reckon we should test it.'

'Sure,' Jeff said cautiously. 'But we'll fight in the open where everyone can see who wins.'

Jeff sat tall and moved his horse on, ensuring that if a beating was to be handed out, he would be the only one on the receiving end of it. Gene shook his head.

'Not now. As Sheriff Armstrong Beck interrupted the last fight, I've arranged a new one. I reckon everyone would enjoy seeing another bout, and this time it'll be a proper fight.'

'Me and you?'

'Yeah.' Gene laughed. 'The deal is: if you beat me I'll know you're a fighter and you can walk away. If you get beaten to a pulp I'll know you fixed the fight and these men will stomp whatever I leave behind into the dirt.'

6

Armstrong Beck had never visited First Creek before. It was a day's travel beyond the boundary of his former county and, it being a peaceful town, he'd never had a reason to look for anyone there.

Maddox Fincher still maintained that his boss was here, giving Armstrong no choice but to play out the situation until he had uncovered the truth. Even if it turned out to be a subterfuge he didn't mind, as he'd expected his mission to be a lengthy one. If he found that Maddox had lied he'd hand him over to the law.

Five miles out of town Maddox veered them to the north. Armstrong contented himself with giving Maddox a long glare, implying that dire consequences were imminent if he was playing a trick.

Maddox appeared unconcerned. He led Armstrong to a trading post, a ramshackle building that was similar to Quentin Saunders' post. Interestingly it had a large barn that put Armstrong in mind of the building in which the illegal fight had taken place.

As they dismounted Maddox cast a furtive glance at the barn, confirming Armstrong's suspicions. He headed straight for the door and peered inside.

Apart from a pile of straw the building was empty, but that in itself was odd.

'Last chance to change your mind,' Maddox said. 'You won't enjoy what's about to happen.'

'I don't scare that easily,' Armstrong told him.

'I do.' Maddox turned to the door and took a deep breath. 'I reckon I'll be as welcome as a rattler in your boot.' He raised an eyebrow, suggesting the reason for his concern would become clear shortly. Then he set off, Armstrong following two paces behind him.

61

As he expected deception Armstrong stopped at the door of the trading post and watched Maddox cross the deserted room to the counter. Maddox trod lightly, as if he hoped he wouldn't be heard, but there came a rustle of movement and a person came up to the counter.

At first Armstrong assumed it was a scrawny man but at a second glance he saw the long red hair and realized that he was looking at a willow-thin woman of around forty. He couldn't help but gulp when he recognized her as Ruth Evans.

He had met her only once, briefly, four years previously when he'd had to tell her that he'd failed to stop her husband, Wardell, from being shot after the Hickory Point boxing match.

Ruth was wearing man's clothing and was wiping her hands on a wet towel. The moment she saw Maddox she came to a sudden halt.

The two of them stared at each other, then Ruth resumed rubbing her hands so vigorously that she seemed in danger of removing skin, while Maddox stood still and cowering.

He was the first to open his mouth to speak, but he had yet to form his first word when Ruth threw the wet towel at him. Maddox jerked away, but it still wrapped itself around his face. By the time he'd peeled it away, she'd come around the counter.

'No excuses,' Ruth said, her voice high-pitched with anger. 'You'll never work for me again.'

'I thought that might be the case, but — ' Maddox didn't get to finish his excuse as she landed a powerful slap on his cheek, such as the fighters of two days ago would have been proud to deliver.

The blow knocked Maddox's hat to the floor. When he bent to retrieve it she kicked his rump and sent him sprawling.

She hadn't noticed Armstrong yet, but he didn't mind as the delay gave him time to think about how he should deal with her and she was giving

Maddox what he deserved.

Maddox crawled across the floor with a hand raised to protect his head, but before he could regain his feet he got a slap on the back and a back-handed blow to his shoulders. Then he hurried to the wall where he stood cringing and wringing his hat.

Ruth didn't hit him again, but that was only because she had returned to the counter to collect a broom, which she swished from side to side as she advanced on Maddox.

The cowering man sized up the broom. Then he decided that now was not the moment to finish his explanations. He ran to the door.

He wasn't fast enough and he got two firm blows to the rump before he gained the door. Armstrong raised his arm to let Maddox pass beneath it. Then he faced the woman with a tentative smile on his lips.

'What are you grinning at?' she demanded, her mildly aggrieved tone suggesting she had yet to recognize him.

Seeing that she now held the broom tilted downwards to the floor, Armstrong turned to check on Maddox. He watched him run on until he reached a horse trough where he used the towel to run water over the back of his neck. He looked cowed enough not to run away, so Armstrong remained standing in the doorway.

When he turned back Ruth was brushing a straying lock of red hair that was tinged with grey away from her eyes. Her hand was shaking; evidently she'd now placed him.

Armstrong gulped to moisten his dry throat.

'It's been a while,' he said.

She searched his eyes, her throat tightening as she struggled to control her emotions.

'I haven't forgotten. How could I after what you did?'

Armstrong took a deep breath, figuring she deserved nothing less than that he speak his mind.

'Except I've never been sure what did

happen back then. Maybe enough time has passed for us to talk and help each other understand the full truth about what happened to Wardell.'

He had meant to phrase his reply as a question, but his sombre tone made it sound like a statement; he watched her grind her jaw, saw her colour rise to match her hair.

With faltering steps, dragging the broom along, she walked up to him. She looked him over, her piercing gaze appearing as if she were memorizing his form.

Then she transferred the broom to the other hand. A moment before she acted Armstrong saw in her eyes that she intended to repeat the treatment she'd meted out to Maddox. As he figured he deserved it he didn't try to stop her.

He had not anticipated that instead of delivering one of the round-armed swipes she'd given Maddox she would swing the broom upwards. It slipped between his legs and kept rising, gaining in speed until the head came to a bruising halt.

His eyes watered so much that the next minute passed in a blur; the all-consuming pain meant he barely felt the blows she rained down on his back as he staggered away from the door, doubled over.

When the pain had receded enough to let him take note of his surroundings again he found that she'd gone back into the post and that he was sitting down, leaning back against the water trough. Maddox was at his side.

'I told you that you wouldn't thank me none for bringing you here,' Maddox said. With a gleam in his eye he offered Armstrong the damp towel.

7

'If I win, I get beaten,' Jeff grumbled for not the first time since yesterday. 'If I lose, we both get beaten.'

Nathan raised his fists and, moving lightly on his feet, he jerked from side to side, bobbing his head up and down.

'Land a punch on me and maybe neither of us will get beaten,' he said.

Jeff bunched his hands, then let them dangle.

'But I don't want to land a punch on you. For that matter I don't want to land a punch on Gene Hansen either.' He shook his hand ruefully. 'When I hit Harris it hurt.'

Nathan stopped jigging about and, setting his hands on his hips, he sought another way to get Jeff motivated for the fight tomorrow night. They had gone 400 yards out of town to practise, picking a depression in the ground that provided a natural ring.

Unfortunately, on the way they had gone past the place where Harris and Keenan had been attacked.

Other than the scuffed ground and some worrying dark patches, there were no clues as to what had happened there. They had not seen the two men since the previous night.

This ought to have spurred Jeff on, but it appeared to depress him even more.

Their only boxing experiences were watching one match and rehearsing moves with Harris to make their bout appear convincing. Prior to that the two friends had often got into scrapes, but saloon-room brawls were different from the formality of a contest between two determined men.

That thought made Nathan smile. Jeff must have noticed his change in mood, as he stood tall.

'If you can't win properly, fight dirty,' Nathan told him with a mock snarl.

'Like we'd do if someone confronted

us on the trail or in a saloon?' Jeff said, brightening.

'That's right. Ignore the rules. Catch Gene off guard. Hit him while he's down.' Nathan matched his words with action as he punched left and right, and then scythed a big kick. 'Kick him in the guts. Stomp on his fingers.'

His suggestions made Jeff nod. A gleam of hope appeared in his eye. Then he thumped Nathan in the stomach, cutting off his litany of tactics.

Nathan folded over in response to the blow, gasping for air, then dropped to his knees and rolled over on to his side. Jeff put a hand up to his mouth.

'Sorry. You got me into a fighting mood.'

'Then at least that's progress,' Nathan gasped between sharp intakes of breath.

He rolled over on to his back while the enthused Jeff carried on sparring, this time with an imaginary partner. Nathan had just decided to stay where he was while Jeff was throwing punches when Deputy Emerson Tate arrived.

Emerson stood on the edge of the depression watching them, a smile on his face. Nathan gestured to attract Jeff's attention; in response Jeff stopped shadow boxing and hauled Nathan to his feet. The two men faced the deputy.

'All this activity must mean that despite the warnings, you're planning to fight on,' Emerson said.

'We're the two least popular men in town,' Nathan told him with a shrug. 'We have to stand up for ourselves.'

'Sheriff Armstrong Beck's last act as a lawman was to save you, so you should know that if you have a problem you bring it to the law.'

Emerson made his way down into the depression. There he regarded them both in turn, his silence giving them the opportunity to volunteer information.

Jeff caught Nathan's eye and glanced at his fists. Slowly he opened them. As Nathan's stomach was still aching he agreed with Jeff's unspoken suggestion that talking to the law was a better option than fighting.

71

'Gene Hansen's arranged another fight tomorrow night,' Nathan said. 'Jeff's taking part in the first bout.'

Emerson glanced away, his eyes narrowing with an emotion that Nathan couldn't work out.

'Details.'

In a faltering voice and with several stops and starts, Nathan described their predicament and the instructions they'd been given: to report tomorrow at the same location as last time. Once he'd gone past the point of no return, he grew in confidence and he gave a full account.

When he'd finished Jeff confirmed his support with a nod. Then the pair of them awaited the lawman's verdict. Emerson kicked at the dirt before making his reply.

'I'm obliged for that information, but it gives me a problem,' he said. 'Do I arrest you for violating Sheriff Livingston Beck's orders when he released you? Or do I give you a chance to redeem yourselves?'

Emerson's stern gaze suggested to

Nathan that the better option might be to go back to jail, but he also figured they'd get as little say with Deputy Emerson as they'd had with Gene.

'We sure would like to redeem ourselves,' he said in a resigned tone.

'I'm pleased. Keep me informed of anything else you learn about this fight and I won't arrest you.'

Both men breathed sighs of relief.

'We're obliged,' Nathan said.

'And we're glad we spoke up,' Jeff added.

'Trusting the law is always the right thing to do,' Emerson said with a sigh of his own. Then he gestured to them to continue practising.

★　★　★

'I know why she hit me, but why was she angry with you?' Armstrong said.

Armstrong and Maddox had taken up a position on a rise 300 yards from the trading post. Since they'd left the post Maddox had been quiet and the tight-lipped look he shot Armstrong suggested he wouldn't be helpful.

'Ruth stages fights in her barn,' Maddox said after a while.

'I thought so,' Armstrong muttered. This confirmed his suspicion that four years ago she hadn't been as surprised that her husband was a fighter as she'd made out.

'Last month I fixed a fight with Harris and Keenan. She wasn't happy about that, so I had to move on.'

Armstrong snorted. 'And you moved on to my town and tried to do the same again.'

'I thought I might get away with it if I went somewhere else and I'd heard Gene Hansen was staging a fight for various businessmen from Lone Gulch.'

'Who helped him organize it?'

'Yardley Weston is Gene's closest aide. There'll be others but I don't know their names.'

'I understand. When you hope to make money you don't ask no questions.'

74

Maddox shrugged. 'I don't. Not that it's helped me.'

'I thought you escaped with the bets?'

'I did, but I had some other debts to repay, and some people from the fight caught up with me.'

'Life never changes for you, does it?' Armstrong said. Maddox scowled, shuffled away and lay prone on the ground, looking down at the post.

'What have you got planned now?' Maddox asked.

'I'll wait,' Armstrong said. 'As a lawman I learnt to be patient. Ruth is involved in organizing boxing matches and when she's calmed down she may give me better leads than you've provided. If she doesn't, this situation will eventually lead me to Vencer Muerte.'

'He hasn't showed for four years. I'm not waiting that long.' Maddox glared at him, but since Armstrong didn't reply he continued: 'Waiting was the right thing for a lawman to do, but if

75

you want results now, you have to make things happen.'

Armstrong frowned, not willing to admit that Maddox was right. He had retired because tracking down the truth about Vencer Muerte was a personal matter that would probably take time and which might require him to violate his sworn duties as a lawman.

Except that since beginning his quest he had behaved in exactly the same way as he had done over the past four years.

He was still struggling to work out how he could make Ruth give him more details about the events of four years ago and wondering whether she might be involved in recent events, when the first visitor arrived.

The rider headed to the post at a slow pace that didn't look suspicious, but Armstrong watched him go in and then come out. This incident marked the first change in the level of activity.

For the next hour as the sun and then the knife-thin sliver of moon set, more riders arrived. They came on their own or in small groups, and, unlike the first man, none of them emerged.

Presently the sounds of laughter and lively conversation drifted up to them.

'I assume Ruth serves a good brew,' Armstrong said.

'She does, but people come here mainly because they can get entertainment at her place that they can't get in town.'

'Then maybe we should join them, provided we can avoid that broom of hers.'

Maddox gulped, his eyes wide and shining with worry in the poor light.

'With the kind of people she attracts, you'll welcome getting only a broom.'

Armstrong shrugged. 'Then tell me more and we won't have to go down there.'

Maddox looked at the post and then at Armstrong, rubbing his mouth in a nervous gesture.

'I reckon that if you hadn't stopped the fight Gene had something else planned that night.'

'Which was?'

'I don't know. I brought you here because Ruth knows more about this secretive world than I do.'

'I'm sure she does, but I don't believe you're as stupid as you look.' Armstrong gave Maddox a long stare. Maddox shrugged.

'You may not know what Gene planned to do for sure,' Armstrong prompted, 'but you can guess.'

Maddox sighed. 'I reckon he planned to stage a second, private fight later that night for a few select guests.'

'Including Vencer Muerte?'

'I reckon he'd have been there.'

'Why would you reckon all that?'

'Because . . . because that's what happened four years ago on the night Grant McClellan died.'

Armstrong smiled, having finally forced Maddox to tell him something useful that he believed.

'And will there be a fight here tonight, either private or otherwise?'

'Not that I know about.' Armstrong

grunted with disbelief. Maddox raised a hand. 'I really don't. She won't confide in me no more.'

'I can't blame her.'

Maddox stood up. He put a hand to his brow and looked down at the post.

'But I do know one thing for sure,' he said. 'Those men are up to something.'

Armstrong followed Maddox's gaze to the post, where forms were moving through the dark. He struggled to discern how many men were scurrying around or what they were doing, but their actions were worrying, as everyone who had arrived earlier had gone inside.

Then, beside the post, a burst of light flared in the night. It quickly faded to a dull glow, then it split up. Points of light bobbed away from the main light.

The sight was puzzling until Armstrong worked out what he'd seen. The men had lit brands and they were spreading out to surround the post.

In seconds the men had formed a circle, their forms standing out as stark shadows behind them. Then they took turns to hurl the brands on to the post's roof.

'Over twenty people are inside,' Armstrong said, aghast as the shingles caught alight.

'And it'll need more than her broom to put that fire out,' Maddox murmured.

8

By the time Armstrong and Maddox had clambered down from the rise the fire had taken hold of the trading post's roof.

The bright flames illuminated the corral, barn and surrounding area, lighting the way for the escaping customers, who were streaming out into the night.

None of them were waiting to see if the others got out; thankfully the arsonists were letting them escape.

Armstrong feared they wouldn't treat Ruth in the same way; sure enough, as he set off running across the flat ground he saw her appear in the doorway briefly. Then she ducked back inside.

When they reached the barn sections of the roof were still undamaged, giving Armstrong hope that they would have enough time to get her out.

'This isn't the time for your tricks,' he said to Maddox. 'Will you help?'

'I don't play tricks,' Maddox said. 'I take bets on illegal games and I always settle my debts, eventually. Helping Ruth should settle my debt to her.'

Armstrong peered around the corner of the barn and saw that six men had attacked her post. He backed away and turned to face Maddox. 'Obliged. We need to act quickly before . . . ' He trailed off and looked again at the raiders, realizing that he recognized many of them.

Before he could start thinking about why Yardley Weston was leading a group of men from Hickory Point Maddox pointed at the corral fence.

'A second door's over there and the fire's not reached that side of the building yet. Only two men are guarding that door, so you keep Yardley occupied and I'll make sure she gets out.'

Armstrong hated taking Maddox's orders, but when he'd forced down the irritation caused by an outlaw speaking to him as a subordinate, he accepted that the plan was a good one. He nodded. Maddox hurried away.

At first Maddox mingled with the customers who in their panic were ignoring the corral and were now running towards the distant town.

The attackers didn't appear to notice him. So, fifty yards away, on the edge of the lit-up area, he veered to skirt around the post until he disappeared in the gloom.

As Armstrong turned his attention on to the gunmen he could do nothing other than hope that Maddox was honouring his promise.

Armstrong faced six men; three were standing in an arc around the front door, two more flanked the second door. Yardley was standing back, overseeing the attack.

Aside from the crackling flames, all was quiet. The men were casting glances around them and moving from side to side as they awaited developments.

Armstrong didn't want to act until he was sure that Maddox was in position. He was only halfway to a count of a hundred, the time he reckoned it would take Maddox to reach the second door, when the watching men swung around.

They all looked in the opposite direction to the way Maddox had gone. A moment later Armstrong saw the reason.

One of the customers had returned.

This man had retrieved his horse and he was galloping full speed towards the line of men. They started scrambling for their guns before they thought better of attempting to shoot him and leapt aside.

They had yet to hit the ground when the rider dismounted in a fluid motion. He landed on the ground in a forward posture and used his momentum to propel him towards the door.

Armstrong moved out from the corner, taking cautious steps, but when the man reached the door without drawing gunfire he speeded up.

He reckoned that Yardley and the others had no reason to suppose that the former sheriff of Lone Gulch would be here, so he stood a good chance of not being recognized. With his head down to further protect his identity, he hurried between the sprawling men.

They looked at him with with some curiosity but, as with the first man, they let him pass unhindered; he reached the door a few seconds after the unexpected helper had slipped inside.

He was confronted with the sight of Ruth and the helper struggling. The man had grabbed her hands and she was trying to wrest herself free of him.

Armstrong's arrival surprised her. She stopped struggling and the man dragged her towards the door.

'Let me go,' she hollered. 'I'm staying.'

'You have to come,' the man said as he drew her on. 'The whole roof's ablaze.'

Hearing these words she looked up at a roof that was seemingly intact, with only a few tendrils of smoke filtering down. She shook her head and dug in her heels, dragging the man to a halt in front of the door.

'Listen to him,' Armstrong said. 'The fire's worse than it looks from in here, but that'll change quickly.'

This proved to be the worst thing he could have said; her eyes narrowed in anger and, with manic energy, she squirmed and kicked at her saviour until she tore herself free.

The two men exchanged exasperated looks. Then, as Armstrong reckoned she wouldn't welcome his manhandling her, he opened the door while the man grabbed hold of her again.

This time he wasn't gentle, using his superior strength to grip her arm firmly. Then he wrapped his other arm around her waist.

Averting his face from the slaps she was raining down on his head and shoulders, he attempted to drag her backwards through the doorway. Ruth, in one more desperate attempt to frustrate his efforts, grabbed the side of the door and hung on, preventing any further progress.

The man kept tugging until her upper body was horizontal, but she'd gained a strong handhold and Armstrong saw that he'd have to move in.

Ruth gave him a warning glare; he ignored it and put a hand over hers as it gripped the doorframe. One by one he raised her fingers until she slipped free.

A volley of gunshots rang out. Ruth gave a strangulated scream and dropped to her knees.

A moment later her unknown saviour stumbled. He keeled over holding a hand to his bloodied back, leaving her lying in the doorway.

Armstrong hurried past her through the door and helped her to her feet. She was uninjured and she didn't try to fend him off. They both got back inside the trading post with no further shots being fired.

Armstrong looked at the wounded man through the open doorway. He wasn't moving, so he closed the door and faced Ruth.

In the short time during which they'd been trying to get outside, sections of the roof had burned through. Flames were now licking at the underside of the timbers. Thick smoke was filling the air, making Armstrong's throat tickle, but Ruth still appeared more aggrieved by his presence than by the impending disaster.

'What did you come back here for?' she demanded.

'Yardley Weston is burning down your post.' Armstrong coughed as the smoke thickened. 'He'll let anyone in, but he won't let you out. Maddox is at the other door. We can get out that way.'

'If I have to rely on you and Maddox to escape, I'd sooner stay in here and burn.'

Despite her comment, she moved towards a door that led into a short corridor. The second door was at the end of it.

The flames hadn't reached this part of the building yet and the corridor was dark, only the light from the main room lighting their way.

As Ruth hurried down the corridor a section of the roof in front of the main door collapsed, slamming to the ground and sending sparks showering in all directions.

A blanket of smoke hit Armstrong. Even though he clamped his lips and eyes tightly shut he still had to cough and blink back tears.

Their only other escape route now being cut off he followed Ruth. He caught up with her as she stopped at the door to listen.

'I'll go out first,' he said, risking taking a breath as the smoke pursued them down the corridor.

'I won't accept your orders,' she snapped.

'This time you have to. Keep behind me and move quickly into the darkness.' When she opened her mouth to retort anger got the better of him and he slapped a hand over her mouth. 'And don't say you'll enjoy seeing me get shot, because if I get you to safety I won't mind that happening.'

She slapped his hand away. 'When you breathe your last, don't go thinking you've righted the wrongs you've done me.'

Her defiant statement lost some of its bite as she then had to cough. Fear replaced the anger in her eyes as she struggled to get her breath.

The glow in the main room was getting brighter and the crackling fire sounded ominously close. Armstrong didn't reply, allowing her the pleasure of having the last word to save them from standing here arguing until the flames reached them.

He drew his six-shooter and swung round to face the door. He stood for several seconds to let her get into position behind him. Then he threw open the door and charged into the night.

He didn't dally to check whether she

had followed; as the smoke billowed around him he kept his head down, looking from the corners of his eyes for the two men who were guarding the door.

After taking five long paces, he picked them out by the fence. These men were watching the fire with hands raised to their brows to protect them from the heat and the dazzling light, but the moment they saw him they snapped guns round to aim at him.

Still running, Armstrong aimed at the nearer man and tore off a wild shot. Both men returned equally wild gunshots, their aim confused by his fast-moving form and the dazzling light from the fire.

His main object being to save Ruth, he had no choice but to try to save himself. He flung himself to the ground, trusting that she would follow her own self-preservation instincts.

He hit the ground on his chest and slid along for three feet. When he came to a halt he dug his elbows in and took aim.

He heard Ruth dive to the ground behind him as he scythed a low gunshot into the thigh of the right-hand man, who jerked away and grabbed hold of the fence to stop himself falling over.

A second shot ensured that that effort would fail. Then Armstrong swung his gun sideways to pick out the left-hand man. His peripheral vision had told him this man already had him in his sights, so he took aim carefully.

His opponent had enough time to fire and his gunshot sliced into the dirt six inches from Armstrong's chin, kicking dust up into his face and eyes.

He shook his head and aimed again, but the dirt and the smoke had blurred his vision and he struggled to pick out his target. The man appeared to be jerking around, so that Armstrong had to blink rapidly until he could focus on him.

He breathed a sigh of relief. His blurred vision had misled him.

Maddox had shot the man, who had been writhing around in his death throes. Before Armstrong could get a clear aim at him, the man tumbled on to his side.

Then Maddox came quickly into view. He vaulted the fence and, looking only towards the front of the trading post, he scurried past Armstrong.

By the time Armstrong had got to his feet Maddox was helping Ruth to stand. She let him aid her that far, although the moment she was standing, she shook off his hands and ran for the fence on her own.

Armstrong nodded his thanks to Maddox and both men hurried after her as she slipped between the rails of the fence.

Then, while Maddox and Ruth ran towards the safety of the darkness, Armstrong stayed to check the progress of the blaze. The front half of the trading post was collapsing and the building was beyond saving, even if anyone were to try.

Yardley and the other men who had been guarding the front door weren't visible, but the gunfire would draw them soon. Armstrong didn't wait for them to arrive. Keeping his head down he ran after the other two.

Ruth's and Maddox's forms became dimmer with every pace, but when they reached the rise they were still visible as dark shapes in the night. Ruth stopped at the bottom and found a rock to sit on, from where she looked back at her property. Moments later Armstrong, breathless now, joined them.

Armstrong reckoned nothing he could say would cheer her and anything he did say would provoke an argument. So he stood to her right while Maddox stood to her left as they awaited developments.

From their position now further away from the inferno they could see people hurrying about; they appeared to be fleeing. Several horses were now loose so it seemed likely that finding a mount for Ruth wouldn't be a problem.

'There's Yardley,' Maddox said, pointing.

Yardley was leading a group of three riders in pursuit of a straggling line of fleeing customers, perhaps under the misguided belief that they included Ruth. The customers' failure to help Ruth didn't make Armstrong feel inclined to help them, and Ruth's snort of derision suggested that she agreed.

'I can take care of myself from here,' she said, her voice gruff and tired.

'I'm sure you can,' Armstrong said, choosing his words carefully. 'But Yardley Weston burnt down your post for a reason. I intend to find out what it is.'

She looked at him with eyes that were bright with despair in the night.

'Four years ago I lost my husband because of you. Now you turn up again, and this time I lose my business and my home.' She stood up and set her hands on her hips. 'So why should I help you?'

9

The evening was quiet and warm, but Deputy Emerson Tate couldn't enjoy it.

Worrying about his orders to keep Livingston away from the fight tomorrow night had made him restless all day and, while he manned the law office, he couldn't avoid dwelling on it.

Livingston had left town in mid-afternoon and had yet to return. He hadn't explained where he was going, which was unusual.

Livingston's instructions were for him to look after the office, but with his thoughts whirling about what his boss might be doing, he locked up the office and set off in search of a distraction.

When he found one he wished he'd stayed in the office.

He had hoped his mysterious informer wouldn't give him any more instructions, as they always turned out to be bad news. So when he saw that the old sign outside Yardley Weston's hardware store had been tipped over, he headed around to the back of the stables in some trepidation.

Having to wait thirty minutes for a response only made him brood. He had forged a decent life for himself in Lone Gulch and until this week he had managed to put his past behind him.

For four years he had done nothing wrong and he'd done plenty that was right. In his own mind, while serving as Armstrong's deputy he'd made up for his one mistake a hundred times over, but now one man who knew what he'd done four years ago could destroy his future.

Despite feeling worried for himself, the worst thing about this situation was that he'd had to mislead first his boss Armstrong and now his friend Livingston. He hoped that at the very least, if the truth did emerge, even if they were unable to carry on as before, Livingston would forgive him.

These thoughts only increased his nervousness; when the stable door edged open he spoke quickly.

'What's wrong?' he croaked, then he coughed and spoke in a calmer tone. 'I have everything under control. You didn't need to risk being seen talking to me.'

'I'll decide what risks I'll take,' the unseen man said, his tone as measured as usual. 'And I wanted to hear your explanation of what your new sheriff has been doing this afternoon.'

'I don't know what Livingston's doing. But he's sure to tell me when he gets back.'

'I can save him the trouble. He's been scouting around Oscar McClellan's old homestead, examining the barn, looking for clues.'

'I followed your instructions and told him I hadn't heard any rumours about further fights, but he's not stupid. He's getting leads from the same informant who helped his father. The best I can do is to act naturally and come up with a distraction tomorrow . . . ' Emerson paused to collect his thoughts, 'unless you're going to tell me that you're worried about all this and so the fight's now been abandoned?'

'You sounded hopeful.' The man waited for an answer that Emerson wasn't prepared to voice, then he chuckled. 'It hasn't been abandoned. But you have to be more careful. Keep your sheriff in line.'

'Livingston tells me what to do, not —'

'I don't care what risks you have to take,' the man snapped, appearing to lose his patience for once. 'Your role is to sort out problems.'

Emerson knew he shouldn't answer back, but being given the impossible task of fooling Livingston while not casting suspicion on himself made him slap the stable wall in frustration.

'I wouldn't have any problems if Gene Hansen had organized this fight properly so that no information leaked out. In fact, I found out where he's holding it without any trouble.'

'It's not your place to question my orders. All you need to know is that if you fail, you'll suffer the consequences.'

'I accept that, but if you hang that threat over me after tomorrow, I'll knock it back at you.'

'I doubt that. You're now a respected, decent man who always does the right thing. Nobody suspects you have a past. So you won't risk defying me when I can destroy you with just two words.'

The door creaked open and Emerson sensed that the man leaned out. Emerson tensed to fight down the temptation he'd resisted so far of turning and seeing the face of the man who'd tormented him for the last week.

'Only two?' Emerson murmured.

'Sure,' the man whispered. 'I only have to tell the sheriff that his deputy was once known as the infamous Vencer Muerte.'

★　★　★

At sunup Ruth spent only a few moments looking at the tendrils of smoke still rising in the distance before she headed to her horse.

Without comment she prepared to leave. Maddox and Armstrong didn't speak to her; when she was ready to go she turned towards First Creek without even acknowledging them.

Maddox and Armstrong exchanged glances. Then they got ready to leave. She had settled into a brisk trot and it took them fifteen minutes to catch up with her.

When they were flanking her she set her gaze resolutely forward but, as Armstrong expected, after a few minutes the strain of ignoring them wore her down and she drew her horse to a halt.

'If I tell you both I'm grateful you saved my life and you don't owe me nothing, will you leave me alone?' she said.

'No,' Armstrong said.

'That's a relief. I didn't want to have

to say it. So just go.'

'We're not leaving you until you're safe.' His offer made her sneer, so he continued: 'News of what happened to your post will have reached First Creek by now. Sheriff Cooper will be looking for you, but Yardley could still be about.'

'He's long gone.'

Armstrong narrowed his eyes. 'You say that with assurance. It makes me wonder if you know why he torched your property.'

She snorted. 'Four years of being a lawman has clearly taught you something, after all.'

Armstrong glanced at Maddox to see if he wanted to speak. His dubious expression matched Armstrong's thoughts about his chances of getting her to reveal anything, and that persuaded the former lawman to make her an honest offer.

'You blame me for your husband's death, but Wardell's demise has gnawed at me, too. It was my worst mistake and I've longed to find out who killed him and why.'

'Not as much as I have.'

Armstrong gave a small smile. 'When I heard the rumour that Vencer Muerte had returned to attend a bare-knuckle fight like the one Wardell fought in — and like the ones I now know you organize — I reckoned I might find his killer. So I handed in my star and I went looking for answers. I'm not asking you to forgive me, but to help me, please.'

The revelation that he wasn't a lawman any more made her raise an eyebrow; then she looked towards town.

'I can't help you,' she said, her voice now sounding resigned. 'I don't know who killed him.'

'I never thought that you did, but his killer could be linked to Yardley Weston.' He waited, but she shook her head. 'Even if he's not, it's a place to start.'

It was her turn to give a fleeting smile. 'The only thing that starting there will get you is a quick death.'

'So be it.'

She glanced a question at Maddox, who nodded briefly, but she still didn't reply for over a minute.

'I put on . . . I used to put on entertainment for people who wanted to enjoy something that was different from what they could get in town. Every month I staged a boxing match and Sheriff Cooper turned a blind eye as long as I kept everyone in line.'

'That was his decision,' Armstrong said, his low tone showing his disgust at a lawman who ignored the law. Ruth shook her head. 'You wouldn't understand, but it worked, until Gene Hansen and his friends started attending. The locals came for the gambling and for the sport, but these men had bloodlust in their eyes; the bloodier the fight the more they liked it.'

'That's the problem with illegal activities; they attract the kind of people you don't want to meet.' He watched her grind her jaw, various obvious retorts clearly on her lips, but before she could voice them he continued: 'So you're saying Gene sent Yardley to burn down your post?'

'I reckon so.'

'I'm surprised Yardley strayed this far from Lone Gulch, and the men from Hickory Point travelled even further.'

'I thought you of all people would understand that they had to come from there.'

The settlement was over the county boundary in Armstrong's former territory; it was just a collection of buildings set up around a convenient place to ford the creek. He'd rarely needed to go that far upriver as the few people who lived there were quiet and dealt with their problems themselves.

But Hickory Point was where, four years ago, Wardell Evans and Grant McClellan had fought until Grant had died.

Armstrong was still searching for the right way to ask her to admit that she knew there was a connection when she moved her horse on. After she'd gone a few dozen yards she turned north towards Hickory Point.

Armstrong judged that with steady travel they could reach there by sundown.

'You didn't ask her why Gene sent Yardley to burn down her post,' Maddox said, edging his horse sideways to draw alongside Armstrong.

'I didn't think she'd answer.'

'She wouldn't, because she doesn't know.'

'How do you know that?'

'Because she didn't hit me again.' Maddox raised the reins as he prepared to follow her. 'An enthusiastic lawman curtailed the last fight, which meant information had leaked out. Clearly Gene blamed me for that and so he punished my boss.'

'Except you aren't the only one who'll suffer when she works out the truth.' Armstrong looked Maddox steadily in the eye. 'I was the enthusiastic lawman who stopped the fight.'

10

'Something's wrong,' Sheriff Livingston Beck said when he joined Emerson. 'I was told the fight's starting at sundown, so people should be heading this way by now, but we've seen nobody.'

Emerson's gaze followed Livingston's as the young sheriff looked around with an exasperated expression on his face.

Completing his orders to keep the sheriff away from the fight while not appearing as if he were deliberately distracting Livingston was tricky. Since Livingston was convinced that a fight would take place, Emerson hadn't planned his subterfuge beforehand, reckoning that reacting to the situations as they arose would appear more natural.

Accordingly, when Livingston had wanted to leave town at noon his deputy had joined him as he scouted around rather than trying to persuade him to stay. Later they had split up to search for townsfolk heading to Oscar McClellan's abandoned homestead.

Livingston ordered him to ignore people he recognized and to waylay anyone he didn't, but now that they'd met down by the creek to compare stories, it seemed that neither of them had seen anyone, acting suspiciously or otherwise.

'I assume Oscar told you the fight would be held here,' Emerson said.

'He did.' Livingston shrugged. 'And if anyone knows where it was to be held, it's Oscar.'

Emerson frowned. 'Then I reckon Oscar lied. We should head back to town.' Emerson looked away, casting his eyes over the deserted terrain, realizing too late that he shouldn't have stated his opinion so forcefully. Even as he'd been speaking he'd heard the eagerness in his tone. When he turned back Livingston was looking at him oddly, confirming that he'd erred.

'Why are you so convinced there

won't be another fight after we stopped one two days ago?'

Emerson smiled, this being a question for which he'd prepared an answer.

'Whoever was responsible for organizing that fight will have moved on. They won't risk holding another one so soon and the information Oscar passed on about another fight was just wishful thinking on the part of the people who were disappointed the last time.'

'I think the more likely explanation is that, with the secret getting out, the fight is now being held somewhere else.'

'I hadn't thought of that.' Emerson gave Livingston a long look, trying to convey that he had only been offering an alternative view to help Livingston to consider all possibilities, but his lies, even though they were small, had made him feel so guilty that his mouth had gone dry.

Livingston was the first to look away. Then the two men turned their gaze to the water flowing past in the creek.

Livingston tapped a fist against his

side in irritation. Emerson feared he was using his father's trick of staying silent and waiting for him to end the silence with an unguarded comment.

The fact that his guilty conscience was making him think that way gave Emerson a sinking feeling and stoked his worst fear: that he was unlikely to see out today with his reputation untarnished.

'What are you not telling me?' Livingston asked after a while. When Emerson couldn't find a reply, he prompted: 'You've been mighty secretive these last few days. Is something on your mind?'

'I guess I'm finding it hard to accept your father leaving so suddenly,' Emerson said, thinking quickly.

'So am I, but you were acting oddly before he left.'

Emerson shrugged. 'If we're talking openly, then I didn't share your father's enthusiasm for stopping men fighting for money; but that won't stop me doing my duty.'

'See that it never does.'

'I understand,' Emerson said in a suitably chastised tone.

With that matter discussed, the two men waited in silence for fifteen minutes after which Emerson judged that Livingston wasn't as tense as before. When the terrain remained indubitably free of people, Livingston turned his horse away from the creek and pointed towards the distant homestead.

'Come on.' His voice was hoarse and he coughed to clear his throat. 'Let's see what we can find at the house.'

'If we do that it could stop any fight happening and we'll never find the people responsible.'

Again, he'd sounded more insistent than he should have, but this time Livingston merely smiled.

'I'll settle for that.'

As Emerson couldn't think of a way to dissuade him from visiting the house, he said nothing as they moved on together.

They covered the five miles to the homestead at a steady trot. At first sight the buildings seemed to be deserted and the two men rode on without caution.

Emerson dismounted first. In the hope that he could persuade Livingston to leave quickly he put on an efficient air as he searched the barn along with the derelict house and dugout. When he returned he shook his head.

'It doesn't look as if anyone has been here today.' Emerson gestured around at the deserted buildings. 'Surely it's too late now to get this place ready for a fight at sundown.'

For the first time Livingston grunted in affirmation of Emerson's opinion, so Emerson set off to search the surroundings, eager now to appear thorough before they left.

Oscar McClellan had abandoned the homestead four years ago and until the fight this week few people had come here. During that chaotic night, hundreds of feet, hoofs and wheels had compacted the dirt to a solid hardpan, but amidst the markings he found a dark patch on the ground.

When he moved closer the area appeared to be a drying patch of water, as if someone had emptied out a water canteen. He saw wheel tracks beside the water stain and when he raised his head to follow them he saw that they headed away from the house. The most commonly used route was the one back to town, but these tracks headed north.

'These tracks are more recent than the others,' Livingston said when he noticed what had interested Emerson.

'And they're the only sign of life we've come across this afternoon.'

Livingston studied the tracks and then nodded.

'They are, although there's nothing north of here except Hickory Point.' Livingston peered into the distance and nodded slowly. 'Four years ago my father investigated a fight at Hickory Point. That's where he first met Maddox Fincher and heard about

Vencer Muerte.' Emerson looked north. If they went there it would be well past sundown before they returned.

'I wasn't a deputy back then,' he said, content to let Livingston give him orders that would allow him to comply with his own instructions while not appearing that he was trying to divert the sheriff. 'But I gather that's what happened.'

They followed the wagon tracks without further comment. While the house remained in view they looked back frequently, but nobody approached it and Emerson started wondering whether anybody would show there after all.

They'd been riding towards Hickory Point for an hour and the sun was dipping behind the low clouds on the horizon when a worrying new thought hit him that made him bow his head.

For the last week he'd been forced to lie to Armstrong and then to Livingston; now it seemed that his contact had also lied to him.

11

'Keep your head down and whirl your fists,' Nathan said. 'If you get knocked down, stay down.'

'That mean look in Gene's eye says it's a when, not an if,' Jeff said, staring unhappily across the ring at his opponent.

'Then just make sure you last for long enough to make this look good.'

'This isn't like the last fight in the barn.' Jeff looked at his hands and clenched them tightly to remove a tremor. He moved over to get a drink of water. 'And I'm not feeling angry or in the mood to fight dirty.'

Nathan cast his friend a smile. Then he tripped him up, sending Jeff sprawling face down.

Nathan waited until Jeff muttered in anger, then knelt down to help him up.

'That make you feel angry enough to

start punching?' he asked when he'd turned Jeff over. Jeff batted the dust from his vest.

'It makes me feel angry enough to punch you.'

Nathan sighed and went to busy himself in their corner, lining up Jeff's equipment of water, a bucket and a towel.

Earlier that day, as requested, they had reported to the abandoned homestead, but only Gene Hansen had been waiting for them. Information had leaked out about the last fight, Gene had reported.

Even though he had sent Yardley Weston to deal with the people responsible, the leak had necessitated a change of venue. Gene had led them to a stable in Hickory Point where the audience was smaller than at the last fight, with only ten men watching.

Unlike the previous rowdy crowd these men were silent and seated. The chairs had been placed at the end of the stables with seven at the back and three pushed forward.

The men who had taken the front seats had done so in a sombre and deliberate manner, as if there was an unspoken protocol about who sat where.

Nathan had asked Gene Hansen who these three men were. Gene had pointed out that at one end sat Guy Atwood, the owner of the stables where Nathan and Jeff had kept their horses.

At the other end sat Zack Snyder, who owned the largest hotel in Lone Gulch, while in the middle sat Philip Winston, the owner of several saloons. So the leading businessmen in Lone Gulch were here and that alone made Nathan feel even more nervous.

Nathan had tried watching them several times, but their impassive gazes had made him uncomfortable.

There were no women and the men were older than those in the previous crowd, although Yardley Weston supervised a group of young, armed men who roamed around beyond the entrance to the stables.

Yardley was looking for trouble coming from outside and the only hopeful element was the lack of money changing hands. As nobody was interested in betting on the match Nathan hoped that nobody would be too concerned about the result.

Presently Gene entered the ring. He called Jeff to the scratch while gesturing to Nathan to stay in his corner.

Gene said nothing until Oscar McClellan took up a position as his second; unlike Nathan he didn't have any equipment and he paid more attention to what Yardley's guards were doing than to the ring.

'Before tonight's main bout we have a grudge match,' Gene announced, facing the audience. 'It will be between myself and the man who annoyed everyone when he tried to fix the last fight in Lone Gulch.'

This statement wasn't a completely accurate account of what had happened, but it made the watching men become animated for the first time.

118

'For this fight London rules will not apply,' Gene continued, raising his voice over the rising noise. 'The only rule is: there are no rules.'

Gene stepped forward while Jeff cast Nathan a worried look. Then, when Jeff was looking elsewhere, Gene kicked his legs from under him, landing him on his back.

Unlike the last time nobody declared that the fall concluded a round and Gene prowled around Jeff's sprawling form, flexing his fists and grinning.

In the corner Nathan winced. Then, as he knew he'd find it hard to watch his friend getting hurt, he looked towards the door.

The scene outside was still; even the guards had turned to watch the fight.

★ ★ ★

'It looks like the fight's happening here,' Livingston Beck said, peering along the edge of the water towards Hickory Point.

'It could be.' Emerson didn't need to feign his uncertainty as he peered at the stables. 'Either way we need to be cautious.'

'Agreed. We sneak up to the town quietly, but the moment we know for sure, we stop them.'

Emerson gulped. 'The two of us can't take on that many dangerous men.'

'We don't know for sure that they are dangerous. It could be the same rowdy bunch of townsfolk as before. Except this time they won't walk away with just a warning.'

Livingston gave Emerson an encouraging slap on the shoulder. Then, as he had done for the last two miles while the pair of them were sneaking up on the town, he ran along the side of the creek with his head down, leaving Emerson to loiter and wonder how he could comply with his orders.

With the sinking feeling that had been coming on for the last few hours now consuming him, he plodded along. Livingston had taken up a position behind the corner of the first building in town when he reached him; he made no comment on Emerson's tardiness as he peered round the side of the stables.

From this angle they couldn't see inside the building, but the light streaming through the open doorway illuminated the other buildings as the horses lined up outside and the sound of chatter confirmed that a popular event was taking place.

The men parading up and down outside were all from Lone Gulch and their demeanour implied that it was an event at which newcomers wouldn't be welcome.

'We have to be careful here,' Emerson said, looking over his shoulder. When Livingston didn't respond he ventured the one comment he thought might delay his taking action. 'I reckon that's what your father would have done.'

'You're a good friend,' Livingston said, moving back from the corner. 'It helps having you around to provide good advice now that my father's moved on.'

This comment was the worst thing he could have said as it rekindled the guilt that Emerson had kept at bay.

'And your father was a good lawman,' he murmured.

'The best.' Livingston sighed wistfully. 'And you're right. He'd be careful by acting quickly and seizing control of the situation.'

Having taken the opposite interpretation of his advice to that which had been intended, Livingston looked at the stables, leaving Emerson feeling helpless to avoid a situation from which he could see no escape.

'What are your orders?' he heard himself saying.

Livingston outlined a plan in which Emerson would stay where he was while Livingston worked his way around several buildings so that he could approach the stables from a different angle.

Emerson didn't listen to the details, as he didn't intend to follow those orders.

Instead, when Livingston turned away, he whispered a quiet plea for forgiveness. Then he drew his gun, turned it round in his grip, and rapped the butt smartly on the back of Livingston's head.

Livingston went down without a sound. Emerson dropped to his knees to check he was out cold, then dragged him away from the building.

When they reached the water's edge he laid his unconscious friend down on soft ground, then he knelt in the shadows beside him to watch the fight that was raging in the stables.

Two men were slugging it out with grim determination. The thud of fist on flesh made him wince and twitch, reminding him of the time four years ago when he'd been Vencer Muerte.

Back then he'd been on the receiving end of blows like these; now the sounds made him gulp to fight back the nausea that burned his throat.

12

During his journey to Hickory Point Armstrong had been convinced that he was wasting his time and the town would be as peaceful as the last time he had visited it two years ago. But a mile out of town, when he first caught sight of the dozen or so buildings, he nodded with approval at Ruth and Maddox.

They drew their horses to a halt and took stock of the bustling small community. Dozens of horses were at the stables and numerous men were out and about, engaged in animated activity.

'What's happening?' Armstrong wondered.

His question hadn't been particularly directed at either Maddox or Ruth, but Maddox it was who spoke up.

'I feared this might happen,' he said, his nervous tone making it sound as if he was being honest.

'Explain,' Armstrong said when he didn't continue, but Maddox looked at Ruth, who sighed before she came up with the answer.

'There'll be a fight here tonight,' she said in a hollow tone. Her gaze darted about the scene; her rapid eye movements showed she was drawing her own conclusions, which she might not be prepared to voice.

'A woman who has staged fights herself shouldn't judge others,' suggested Armstrong.

She shrugged, her subdued reaction suggesting that the more important matter on her mind was whether this helped to explain what had happened to her husband.

'I never staged fights like this one. I hated dealing with the men who came to my fights with bloodlust in their eyes, but I saw enough to know they weren't satisfied and that meant that others like Gene Hansen could give them what they wanted.'

'Which was?'

'My matches were illegal, but they still had rules.' She glanced at Maddox, who had the grace to look away. 'Some men want to see matches that have no rules.'

'You mean contests where men fight until one of them is killed?'

She coughed before she replied and then it was in a small voice, suggesting that her mind was on the events of four years ago.

'Yes,' she breathed. She looked at Maddox who, in a rare burst of honesty, nodded too.

'I've only ever seen one of those fights,' he said with a gulp. 'I never want to see another.'

'So the fight I stopped two days ago would have been followed by one of these fights to the death,' Armstrong said. 'And that's what'll happened here tonight?'

'If you stopped the last fight, that probably explains why Gene sent Yardley to deal with me,' she said slowly; clearly she was figuring out the situation.

126

When she glared at him Armstrong was tempted to deflect her ire by pointing out Maddox's roles both recently and four years ago, but he resisted the temptation as two riders were approaching. They were a quarter-mile away and coming down a small rise, which suggested that they had been positioned there on lookout.

When the riders were thirty yards away he recognized them as having been amongst the men who had torched Ruth's trade post last night. Ruth raised her chin defiantly while Maddox stared at the riders with wide-eyed concern.

'What happened to your post was a warning to keep out of our business,' the nearer of the riders called when they drew up. 'Move on and don't cross us again.'

Maddox lowered his head, presumably hoping that he wouldn't be recognized. Armstrong started to speak but Ruth spoke over him.

'I'm not moving on until I've agreed a deal to stop you interfering in my business again,' she said.

'No deals, ever. You know the way it works.'

'Except I have something to offer to prove my good intentions.' She pointed at Armstrong. 'I'm sure you've heard of Armstrong Beck, the former sheriff of Lone Gulch and the man who ruined the last fight.'

Armstrong cast Ruth an aggrieved glare, then he jerked his reins to the side, meaning to beat a hasty retreat. Before he could move off both riders drew their guns. They levelled them on his chest, forcing him to raise his hands.

'We know all about you,' one rider said. 'You will come with us.'

★ ★ ★

'How many fingers am I holding up?' Nathan asked, spreading two fingers before Jeff's battered face.

'What fingers?' Jeff murmured staring into the middle distance.

'The ones on the end of my hand,'

Nathan persisted, waggling them.

'What hand?'

Nathan sighed and dragged Jeff to his feet. He put an arm around his shoulders and supported his weight on the way back to their corner. Then, while he collected the water bucket, he left him standing hunched over with his legs spread wide apart.

The moment he released him, Jeff had toppled over and crashed to the ground on his back, so Nathan contented himself with raising Jeff's head and emptying the water over his forehead.

Jeff grumbled a complaint about his treatment, but he did nothing to stop it other than to wave at the water stream with a vague batting motion that carried on even after Nathan had stopped pouring.

This reaction was worse than on the previous five times he'd been pummelled to the ground although, unlike the previous times, on this occasion Gene had relented in his onslaught and declared a break.

Sadly, he'd done this only to give himself a break. Now he was in his corner with a foot raised to rest casually on an upturned bucket while he enjoyed a glass of beer and chatted amiably with Oscar.

Gene showed concern only when he glanced at the audience, most of whom were ignoring the contest. When Gene had downed his drink he nodded at Jeff's corner.

'We're starting again,' Nathan said, leaning down to pat Jeff's arm.

'Four,' Jeff said.

'Four what?'

'You're holding up four fingers.' Jeff held up a hand to demonstrate, although he managed only three fingers. Nathan locked hands with him and tugged.

'Close enough.' Nathan stood Jeff upright. Then he pointed him towards the scratch and gave him a push of encouragement. 'One more knock down and then stay down.'

'Him or me?' Jeff murmured as he made his uncertain way towards the centre of the ring. He didn't reach it.

Gene moved forward to stand in front of him. When Jeff came close enough he planted a palm on his chest and with a contemptuous gesture he tipped him over.

The moment Jeff hit the ground Gene was on him. He dragged him to his feet leaving him standing bent double. Then he slammed two bunched fists down on the back of his neck.

Jeff hit the ground chin first with his body still bent so that his hips were off the ground. Gene kicked him over on to his side and then stood over him waiting for him to get to his feet, but Jeff lay where he'd fallen.

Whether that was because he was following Nathan's instructions or because he had reached the end of his resilience, Nathan couldn't tell, but Gene didn't appear to care as he tapped a foot against his chest encouraging him to rise.

So far Gene had remained silent, but when Jeff didn't get up he started muttering a litany of contempt.

'You're no fighter,' he said. 'You only won before because you fixed the fight. A lot of people lost money, so now you're paying the price.'

The taunting angered Jeff enough to move, but the moment he tried to raise himself, Gene kicked him down again and continued with the accusations.

For the first time the watching men murmured encouragement. Luckily everyone demanded that Gene should finish the fight quickly, so Nathan waved, trying to attract Gene's attention, but the man showed no sign of stopping proceedings.

Jeff again levered himself up; this time he got to his knees before Gene bent down to deliver a swinging punch to his cheek that rocked his head back. Jeff swayed, but Gene didn't let him topple over.

He hurried behind him and grabbed a fistful of hair. He yanked Jeff's head back. Then he swung his fist downwards and flattened his nose.

Blood sprayed and hair tore as Jeff

went down. This time he didn't make a sound; he just lay still.

Gene waited for movement, but when Jeff made none he reached down, grabbed his head again, and repeated the action.

Jeff slammed down on his back with a dull thud, his lack of reaction suggesting that Gene had punched an unconscious man, but that didn't stop Gene from raising him up again.

That sight was enough for Nathan. Determined now to stop the fight he stormed out from his corner. His action drew the biggest reaction so far from the audience but, sadly, it was one of derision.

The laughter spurring him on, Nathan walked up to Gene, who stood his ground with an amused gleam in the eye that only annoyed Nathan even more. Then, from the corner of his own eye, Nathan saw the reason for Gene's cheerful confidence a moment before Yardley Weston ran into him.

Yardley wrapped his arms around

Nathan's chest and drove him on across the ring until Nathan's legs slipped from under him and he went sprawling on to his back. Yardley went down with him and, as they landed, he thrust a shoulder into Nathan's stomach, making him grunt with pain.

Lying pole-axed, he could do nothing to stop Yardley hammering several quick punches into his ribs before he raised himself off him. Then Yardley walked around him, waiting for him to get up.

Nathan took his time and took deep breaths, but a prod and a kick to his ribs forced him to roll away from the blows and get up. He staggered, so moving himself away from Yardley and gaining time to right himself.

The audience's derision was now deafening; the cries seemed to make the blood race through his veins. So, when he saw Gene about to pummel the seemingly comatose Jeff again, he shook himself and charged at Yardley.

He pounded on for four long paces,

then whirled his arms in a berserk action that threw five punches in a matter of seconds. He landed two blows on his opponent, but Yardley blocked the rest with his arms.

Then, when Nathan tired, Yardley stepped up close and thudded a low punch into his guts that caught him in the same place as he'd been hit before.

He folded over while a dull pain made him cough and splutter. Then a fierce uppercut to the chin stood him straight and a follow-up punch to the ribs toppled him over on to his side.

Lacking the strength to fight back, he curled up and willed the pain to subside before Yardley attacked him again.

Fortunately Oscar bade Yardley to return to the door. Even better, Gene stepped away from Jeff.

This action drew a round of applause and, when Nathan was able to make out what the audience was saying he heard only encouragement for Gene to adjudge the fight over. He also heard enough to gather that the derision had been voicing dissatisfaction with the quality of the contest, not with his own performance.

So, his hopes soaring that the torment had ended, he crawled over to Jeff. His friend was barely recognizable: his bloodied face puffy and his lips torn.

The sight helped him to overcome the pain of his own injuries. When he had forced himself to his feet he dragged Jeff out of the ring.

He chose a spot in the endmost stall, close to the open door where he hoped the cool night air would revive Jeff. Then he fussed around him with a wet towel, unsure which injury to deal with first.

He kept his head down and ignored the debate Gene was having with several audience members, making the point that no matter what they decided, for Jeff the fight had finished. Despite this resolution, he still took a deep breath when Gene headed back into the centre of the ring.

'With my opponent unable to continue, the first match of the night is over,' Gene declared.

'At last,' Philip Winston, the saloon owner, shouted to a round of grunted agreement.

Nathan heard footfalls approaching and he looked up to find that Gene had arrived. He had barely a mark on his face.

'Everyone now knows you fixed the fight,' Gene said, folding his arms.

Nathan gestured at Jeff's bloodied form.

'And does this satisfy you?'

Gene cast Jeff a long look, appraising the damage. His expression was stern, as if he'd expected to get something more out of the situation.

'That depends on whether you've learnt your lesson.'

'This world isn't for us,' Nathan said with assurance. 'We're moving on now.'

'That's yet to be decided,' Gene said.

Leaving Nathan to consider that ominous statement, he walked away along the side of the stalls, Oscar following on behind.

Nathan waited until he was sure they wouldn't return before moving to take Jeff outside. When he turned to the door he saw that he wasn't the only person who was relieved Gene had gone.

Maddox Fincher and a woman had arrived. They were standing by the door watching Gene.

When Gene had reached the audience on the other side of the ring they came into the stall. Nathan glared at Maddox but the woman looked at Jeff with horror; a murmured suggestion from Maddox that she should stay back identified her as Ruth.

'It looks as if you got what you deserved,' Maddox said to Nathan.

'While you avoided paying for it,' Nathan snapped. 'We got beaten while you got away with the money.'

Nathan shoved Maddox aside and took Jeff's shoulders, but Maddox leaned towards him.

'You may hate me,' he said, lowering his voice, 'but believe me when I say I never intended anything like this to happen.'

'That doesn't change nothing.' Nathan glanced around cautiously. Yardley had returned to guard the door, from where he was looking at him and Jeff, as were the men who had brought the newcomers. 'But you have one chance to make amends. Get us out of here.'

Maddox winced. He knew that Nathan was right; they were in a dangerous situation and Nathan and Jeff would have to be got away. He glanced at Ruth, who took a moment to consider, then nodded.

'I'll do that, but you'll have to leave Jeff here,' he said.

'Never!' Nathan spluttered. 'Without my help he could die.'

'You're no doctor. Without your help he'll recover in his own time, but if you stay with him you'll both surely die.'

'How do you know that?'

'Because I reckon history is about to

repeat itself and it's something I don't want to happen again ever, to anyone.'

'I don't understand,' Nathan said. He looked anxiously at Jeff. 'And I don't trust you.'

Ruth and Maddox turned to each other. With facial expressions alone they appeared to debate what they should say, but before they had reached a conclusion Gene returned to the ring.

'And now we move on to the bout you've been waiting for,' he declared in the now silent stables. 'Two men, both fearsome boxers, both dedicated to fighting for their lives, will do battle here tonight for a prize of two thousand dollars.'

Enthusiastic applause sounded as two men came through a second door at the other end of the stables. Both men were huge, making Harris Twain seem as puny as Harris had made Jeff look.

'Come with us before the fight starts,' Maddox urged.

Nathan shook his head. With an annoyed wave, he indicated that they should move aside so that he could take Jeff outside before the fighters' seconds took up their positions.

Then he noticed these men didn't have seconds.

'This fight will have no rounds, no breaks, no rules other than the only one that matters,' Gene said. 'Tonight, one man will live and one man will die.'

A roar of approval sounded. As the noise went rippling on, Maddox grabbed his arm.

'You've heard enough to know I'm telling the truth,' he urged. 'Leave now with us, or you'll never leave.'

13

'Are you all right?' Livingston asked, shaking Emerson's shoulder.

Emerson grunted before he raised himself slightly.

'Sure,' he murmured. He uttered only the one word, as saying anything more might make his attempt to sound groggy unconvincing.

'I reckon we were both knocked out. I've been awake for a few minutes, but I couldn't rouse you.'

Emerson knew that. He'd spent the last fifteen minutes, as Livingston returned to consciousness, lying curled up on his side with his eyes closed, trying to look as if he too had been knocked unconscious.

Continuing the charade, he blinked and rubbed his head. He felt relieved that, as the lights had been extinguished in the stables, his attempt to act dazed might not be obvious. Livingston was still dazed and wasn't paying him much attention.

Moving gingerly, Livingston got to his feet. Then he shuffled down to the water's edge where he knelt and threw water on his face.

Emerson came beside him and, moving slowly, he dribbled water over the back of his neck.

'What do you remember?' he asked.

Livingston raised himself upright to consider his reply.

'We'd split up and I was trying to get a better view of the stables, but someone must have sneaked up on me from behind.'

'Same for me.' Emerson turned to look at the stables. 'But it seems that whatever was happening in there has ended now.'

'It has.' Livingston frowned. 'Come on. Let's see what we can find out.'

Emerson nodded. He moved quickly to get into step behind Livingston, content now to let his friend take the lead and for him to be seen to do his duty without complaint.

Livingston noted his enthusiasm with a smile as they headed to the stables where a single light had been left burning in the corner of the building.

It illuminated a space that was empty except for two men who lay in the centre of a marked-out ring. Livingston hurried over to them and turned one man over. He recoiled in shock.

'Dead?' Emerson asked, moving over to the second man.

'Yeah,' Livingston said with a catch in his throat. 'He looks like he's been trampled in a stampede. This was no normal fight. This was slaughter.'

Emerson could have educated Livingston by telling him this wasn't the worst he had seen men do to other men under the guise of competition. But to avoid betraying himself he remained standing over the second man.

'This one's still breathing.'

'Then he'll get justice.' Livingston turned the second man over, narrowed his eyes, then raised his eyebrows in surprise. 'I reckon this is the man we locked up a few days ago.'

Emerson looked more closely at the man's face. His cheeks were bruised and bloodied, his eyes so puffy that Emerson doubted he could see, but he reckoned Livingston had been right.

Then, with a gulp, he understood what had happened here this night.

'Yeah, that's Jeff Morgan,' he murmured, his voice catching.

Livingston clenched a fist in irritation. 'We let him go because he claimed he was no fighter, but he was lying.'

Emerson nodded. Then the sinking feeling that had never been far away for the last few days overcame him and he dropped to his knees.

★ ★ ★

'What do you want?' Armstrong Beck asked.

The dazzling morning light was shining through the open doorway that framed his captor's outline, making Armstrong glance away as the man removed his gag. But when the man moved away from the light Armstrong had no difficulty recognizing him.

'Are you surprised?' Oscar McClellan asked.

'I'm only annoyed with myself for trusting the information you fed me. But that won't matter none if Vencer Muerte showed tonight.'

'He was there, but not in the way you expected.' Oscar sneered. 'But I find it annoying that you've spent so much time trying to work out who killed Wardell Evans and yet you've not worked out even the simplest detail.'

Armstrong looked aloft as he tried to figure out what Oscar's intentions were. The movement left him in no doubt that the ropes that secured his wrists behind his back remained as secure as they had been made when he was captured.

He had been bound, gagged and hooded for most of the time since, but he knew he'd been moved away from

Hickory Point. The length of the journey and the identity of his captor suggested he was being held captive at Oscar's abandoned homestead.

The room in which he was being held was secure and, if he was right about his location, nobody would have a reason to go there.

'Direct your anger at Wardell Evans, the man who beat your son to death.' Armstrong waited for Oscar to incriminate himself, but when he didn't reply, he prompted: 'Then again, I assume you did that four years ago.'

'I didn't kill Wardell, but I've made sure his wife suffered, along with Maddox and all the rest who were involved in killing my son.'

'You mean you set us all up against each other.'

Oscar nodded. 'All I had to do was whisper a few words here and a few words there to the right people. Now Gene is hell-bent on destroying Maddox and Ruth because he reckons they leaked information, while Maddox and Ruth want to destroy you because they think you're to blame, and you want to destroy Gene.'

'Except none of us were directly responsible for your son's death.' Armstrong smiled thinly. 'Vencer Muerte did it, and yet you didn't confront him tonight. If he'd killed my son I wouldn't have let him walk away.'

Oscar walked to the door and peered through a gap in the wood.

'Revenge is odd,' he said after a while. 'It took me two years to find out why my son died, and another two to win Gene Hansen's trust. But now, with my plan to destroy you all developing perfectly, I'm appreciating only the beauty of how fortune and planning have come together, and not the revenge itself.'

'I understand.' Armstrong raised his voice. 'It's better to let justice take its course by telling the law every — '

Oscar rounded on him, his eyes flaring as his brief reflective mood exploded.

'I can't do that when the law failed my son,' he roared. 'When you failed him.'

'And so you reckon that killing me will avenge Grant's death?'

'It won't. That's why I've decided to destroy your son so you can understand how I suffered. Last night Livingston arrived in Hickory Point after the fight ended. Now he's returning to Lone Gulch carrying the seeds of his destruction, just as you did four years ago.'

'Stop talking in riddles!' Armstrong snapped; the mention of his son had destroyed his composure.

Oscar left the doorway and walked over to him. He stood silently for a while, his expression calm as he contemplated the former lawman.

'Then I'll speak plainly. Vencer Muerte isn't a name: it's a title. Ten years ago a Mexican boxer fought in a special bare-knuckle fight. He declared that he would vencer a la muerte: conquer death itself. He lost and so the title of 'Vencer Muerte' was given to the winner.'

'Wardell Evans killed your son and he

became 'Vencer Muerte',,' Armstrong said. He nodded. 'Now another man has earned that title?'

'He has but, as I said, Wardell didn't kill my son. In Hickory Point you saw only what you were supposed to see, just like your son did tonight. He too will learn the lesson of what happens when you jump to conclusions, and I'll make sure it destroys him.'

Armstrong considered these words for some moments; then he nodded.

'Two men are found at the scene of a staged fight. One man is beaten and killed and the other man is beaten and injured. It seems obvious that the injured man killed the dead man, except that the injured man was hurt beforehand, leaving the victor, this Vencer Muerte, to sneak away unseen. Later the injured man is killed to preserve the secret.'

'So you've finally worked it out.' Oscar spread his hands. 'When a successful Vencer Muerte emerges, Gene needs to explain how the victims died, especially when they're local men. The current champion is particularly fearsome.'

Armstrong shrugged, which drew Oscar's attention to his bonds.

'Your son or Maddox Fincher could have told me the truth. Clearly they were too scared to speak.'

Anger flashed in Oscar's eyes. He grabbed Armstrong's gag.

'Your son won't fare any better when faced with the same situation. He arrested an injured man, presuming him to have killed the dead man. If he works out what happened, he'll be killed. If he doesn't work it out, his prisoner will be killed and that failure will ruin him.' Oscar raised Armstrong's gag. 'I hope you enjoy waiting for news.'

'My son's resourceful,' Armstrong shouted while he could still speak. 'No matter what traps you've laid, he'll rise to the — '

Oscar wrapped the gag around Armstrong's mouth, curtailing his taunts. He stood back to consider his handiwork, then turned to the door.

'Either way, when I return, I'll kill

you.' Oscar threw open the door and glanced around outside. Then he looked back at Armstrong. 'Don't think about escape. Gene Hansen is on guard outside. If you take one step through this door he'll kill you.'

14

'Gene and Yardley aren't doing any-thing,' Nathan said. 'So we need to work on a plan to free Jeff.'

Maddox gestured at him to be silent while Ruth muttered something under her breath. All day they had watched the homestead where Nathan's and Jeff's troubles had started.

Earlier that morning four men had been there, but later one man had left for Lone Gulch and another man had gone north towards Hickory Point. Gene Hansen and Yardley Weston were still around, wandering in and out of the barn or lounging around in the derelict house.

From their position on a rise 250 yards away, Nathan couldn't tell what they were waiting for.

'If you're bored, go into Lone Gulch and ask the sheriff to release him,' Ruth said.

Maddox snorted a laugh and Nathan shuffled away from his companions, feeling suitably chastised.

Despite his asking several times they hadn't explained why he'd had to leave Jeff, nor what they planned to do. But he knew they were taking on ruthless men so, after seething silently for a while, he joined them in watching the buildings.

'I don't care how risky what you're planning is, I want to help,' he declared.

'You were doing that when you were being quiet,' Ruth told him.

Nathan slapped the ground in frustration. 'If you won't tell me what's going on, I'll go down to the house and talk to Gene.'

'That's a good idea. It'll give him someone else to shoot up.'

Nathan looked aloft in exasperation; Ruth shook her head sadly, leaving Maddox to speak.

'Gene works for the mayor,' Maddox said in a weary tone. 'But the mayor doesn't know he organizes boxing matches where the loser is beaten to death. Somehow we have to come to a deal with him.'

Nathan gulped. 'How can you negotiate with a man like that?'

'By giving him what he wants,' Ruth said. 'I'll agree to work for him and help him organize another fight, and this time I'll make sure nobody finds out about it.'

'Last night we placated Gene,' Maddox said. He glanced at Ruth; she lowered her gaze, confirming they wouldn't tell him the details. 'So he didn't kill us on sight, but it's still a gamble as to whether he'll hear us out today.'

Nathan nodded. 'So what are you waiting for?'

'Now that's the first sensible question you've asked today,' Ruth said.

Maddox uttered a resigned sigh. Then they both stood up.

'I guess it's either now or never,' Maddox said.

She smiled; then, without further

comment, they moved down the rise.

Nathan kept his head lowered as he watched their progress. They had covered a dozen paces when Gene noticed them. He beckoned Yardley to meet them while he walked behind the barn.

When they arrived at the homestead Maddox took the lead, standing a few paces ahead of Ruth as he faced Yardley. With much animated waving of his arms Maddox outlined their offer. Then Ruth stepped up to join him and continued with the story.

Even when it appeared that he had heard the full explanation Yardley just stood impassively. Maddox and Ruth looked at each other and shrugged, clearly his silence was making them uncomfortable.

When they turned to look at him again it was to face a drawn gun. Maddox backed away, raising his hands in a warding-off gesture; Ruth stepped forward.

Neither move helped them as rapid

gunfire tore out. Maddox and Ruth jigged from side to side as lead sliced into the ground around their feet.

With gunshots still blasting out Maddox grabbed Ruth's arm and tried to drag her away, but she stood her ground and shook him off. Then, despite the gunfire, she advanced on Yardley.

That proved to be a mistake when Yardley raised his gun from its downward position and fired. Nathan couldn't see where the shot hit her, but she crumpled over. Then she dropped to her knees.

Maddox hurried towards her but Yardley's rapid gunfire hammered into the ground between them, forcing him back and, worse, Ruth tipped over to lie on her side. She didn't move again.

Maddox watched her, holding a hand to his mouth; his shock was obvious even to Nathan. Then, with a visible wrench, he turned on his heel and ran.

He made for the barn but gunfire splayed across the side of the building, forcing him away. Then Yardley moved closer and, no matter which way

Maddox ran, he fired into the ground before his feet, forcing him to backtrack.

Nathan hated watching him being toyed with, but he could do nothing to help.

After trying to flee in several directions, Maddox moved past Ruth's body. In a sudden change of mind he slid to a halt and turned to face his tormentor.

He stomped his feet to show that he did not intend to provide Yardley with any more sport. Yardley shrugged and raised his gun. With two quick bursts of fire he shot Maddox in the chest.

Maddox collapsed to the ground beside Ruth. He twitched. Nathan was 250 yards away, so it might have been his imagination but he reckoned Maddox placed a hand on her shoulder before he stilled.

Nathan stared at the scene, aghast. Maddox had helped to get him into this mess in the first place, but last night he and Ruth had taken him away from a bad situation and protected him.

He shook himself and turned away, meaning to go for his horse and ride to Lone Gulch. But he'd yet to take a single step when he saw that Gene Hansen had sneaked up on him.

Gene was looming over him with his gun drawn and his gaze narrowed to streaks of ice.

'Your turn to run,' he said.

15

The sign outside Yardley Weston's hardware store had been placed upright again.

Emerson kicked it aside and glared down the main drag, trying to fight down his irritation. He failed.

He had told his tormentor that last night was to be his final task. Despite several tricky moments he had completed it, now he reckoned that the outcome that this man had wanted had been achieved.

Jeff Morgan had been arrested on presumption of having killed another man in an illegal fight and Livingston was now collecting proof that the intention had been to fight to the death. He wasn't considering any alternative explanations.

Eager to get an uncomfortable encounter over and done with, Emerson trudged round the stables and stood at the back door. He didn't have to wait for long before the door was inched open.

'You did well,' the familiar voice said.

'I'm pleased, but only if I did well enough to mean I never have to meet you again,' Emerson replied, unable to keep the anger from his tone.

'I've almost finished with you.'

Emerson had expected this answer, but he still opened and closed his fists three times before he spoke again.

'That doesn't matter none to me because I've finished with you.'

'Then I hope you're ready to deal with the consequences after everyone learns the truth about you.'

Emerson took a deep breath and half-turned towards his tormentor. Although he still kept his eyes averted, he sensed that the man was backing away from the door.

'Even if I do your bidding again you could use that threat for ever,' said Emerson. 'There has to be an end to this, and that moment came last night when I delivered what you wanted.'

'You don't know what I want. This is just the start of my plans to make — '

The man didn't complete his explanation as Emerson roared with anger and swung round to kick the wall. He glared at the gap in the doorway, but the raging anger that he had kept in check for the last week, and which had once brought him success, didn't fade away.

He hurled himself at the door and stormed into the stables, his blood pounding with assurance that fighting back was the right course of action. He picked out his tormentor, who had put an arm to his face to hide his identity and was now backing away along the wall.

Emerson caught up with him and yanked the arm down. He had met this man before, but in his present angry state it took him a few moments to recall when that had been.

'You're Oscar McClellan,' Emerson then murmured in surprise, 'Grant's father.'

'The man you killed when you earned the title of Vencer Muerte.'

Oscar shook Emerson's hand away.

'The contest was for money. Grant knew the result of failure, as did I. There was nothing personal in what we were both prepared to do.'

Oscar backed away for another pace and waved an angry hand at him.

'That's no comfort when you survived and my son didn't, and when you're now a respected deputy lawman and nobody knows about your past.'

'I don't care what you've done to me. You lied to Armstrong and then Livingston, feeding them information while giving me different details.'

Oscar chuckled. 'It sure was easy to set you all against each other.'

Emerson waved a dismissive hand at him and half-turned to the door, appearing as if to walk away. Then, in a rapid movement that had once been effective in catching his opponents off guard, he swung back.

He had planned to hit Oscar's cheek

with a back-handed swipe, but Oscar reacted quickly and jerked away from the intended blow. Emerson changed the thrust into a lunge for the man's throat.

He gripped Oscar's neck. Then, as his first positive action made his blood race again, he brought up his other hand to tighten the stranglehold.

'This is for what you people did to Jeff Morgan,' Emerson muttered as he squeezed. 'He's a good man, but all your whispering got him beaten to a pulp and now he's been charged with murder to cover up your dirty secret.'

Oscar brought up his his hands to grasp Emerson's wrists. He tugged, but Emerson locked his fingers together and Oscar couldn't loosen their hold. As Oscar's eyes bulged and his complexion became suffused, Emerson walked him backwards and pressed him against the wall. Oscar made a pitiful gurgling sound in his constricted throat and waved his hands ineffectually.

Those movements became weaker but Emerson still gripped him tightly.

His eyes became unfocused and he let raw anger consume him.

For how long he kept his hands locked around Oscar's neck he wasn't sure. But when with a shudder he became aware of his surroundings again, Oscar's head had lolled to one side and a dribble of bloody drool dangled from his lips.

Emerson flicked his hands open, making the fingers creak after his exertions.

As horror at what he had done made Emerson take an involuntary step backwards, Oscar slid down to sit with his back against the wall, staring ahead with unseeing eyes, his secrets and his plans lost for ever. Emerson regarded him for some moments, then with a snort of derision he kicked him over.

'You took on a fighter,' he muttered, standing over him. 'And the thing about us fighters is, we fight back.'

Emerson chuckled, but his attempt to liven up his spirits didn't cheer him and so he put his mind to practical matters.

He could never tell anyone why he'd killed Oscar, so to continue fighting back he needed to get the body out of town and dispose of it somewhere where nobody would ever find it.

His thoughts turned to the wagon owned by the law office. They rarely used it; it stood in the corner of the stables hemmed in by other rarely used equipment.

He reckoned it would take a while to get it out, so first of all he he needed to hide the body away in the back of the wagon.

Working quickly he dragged Oscar's body across the stables and tipped it over the sideboard. He threw a horse blanket over it and then he looked around for items to lay on top of the blanket and so keep the body disguised from prying eyes.

He had yet to find anything suitable when foot-falls sounded behind him, making him turn. Livingston was standing in the doorway, looking around the stables with quick darting glances that suggested he'd been searching for Emerson for a while.

'What are you doing back there, Emerson?' Livingston asked, his tone light and conversational.

Emerson stretched those fingers that a few minutes ago had throttled Oscar McClellan, trying to force down the anger that had driven him on so that he could reply calmly.

'I was thinking of using the wagon to scout around.'

'Why?'

Emerson gulped, lost for an answer. When Livingston came inside and moved towards the wagon Emerson hurried towards him to intercept him, then veered away in a sudden change of direction, finding he had to get outside.

'I need fresh air,' he said as he moved past Livingston.

He heard Livingston turn on his heel and kept going until he reached the open doorway; there he held on to the door and doubled over, as if he were about to vomit.

His relative success at play-acting last night told him not to overplay his performance. So he looked downward, dragging in long breaths while he waited for Livingston to join him.

'You're whiter than a summer cloud,' Livingston said, looking at him with concern. 'What's wrong?'

Emerson rubbed the back of his head. 'I reckon it's that knock I got on my head last night. This morning I feel tired and faint.'

'I feel fine, but then again I've always reckoned I have a thick skull.' Livingston leaned back against the door, rubbing the back of his own head. 'But we're making progress, so take a rest.'

'We've arrested one man, but whoever organized that fight is still free.' Emerson felt his forehead. Then he looked at the dry hand and curled his lip, as if he'd discovered he had a temperature. 'But you're right. I won't push myself. That's why I'd decided to ride around on the wagon so I could lie down in the back if I felt ill.'

His explanation sounded weak even to his own ears; Emerson couldn't meet

Livingston's eye but Livingston nodded.

'That's a good idea.' Livingston pushed away from the door. 'I'll help you move it outside.'

'No!' Emerson snapped, halting Livingston. He lowered his voice. 'Don't treat me like an invalid. I'm trying to take my mind off the pain.'

'All right,' Livingston said, looking at him sceptically for the first time. He pointed out of town. 'When you're ready, find and question Gene Hansen. He was seen leaving town yesterday and this morning he was sporting bruises.'

Emerson smiled. 'You can trust me,' he said.

16

Gene Hansen was getting closer.

The moment Nathan had seen that he was trapped he had run. To his surprise he had got away without Gene attempting to shoot him, so, with his head down, he'd headed for the nearest cover: the bed of a dried-up rill.

Only when he'd scrambled into safety did he accept that Gene and Yardley liked games and that, like Maddox Fincher earlier, he'd been allowed to run to provide entertainment. He didn't mind as long as he got away, but when he raised his head to survey the terrain, that possibility seemed remote.

Gene was coming down the rise while Yardley was moving to intercept him with assured strides that showed they knew where he was.

When they had left the homestead

they had given him a possible route to safety: getting to the buildings, stealing a horse, and beating a hasty retreat. He was also aware that this might be what they wanted him to do, so as to prolong the chase, but he figured he didn't have a choice.

On hands and knees and with his head down Nathan scurried along the rill-bed. He didn't dare look up for fear of revealing his exact position but when he reckoned he was level with the buildings he rolled up on to the ground.

Then, with his head down, he ran for the barn. He didn't stop to check where his pursuers were and he reached the back of the building without being fired upon.

From here he could see down the length of the barn; beyond it lay Maddox and Ruth, their bloodied forms quite still. Nathan lowered his head for a moment, then he set off down the side of the barn, the sight of the bodies spurring him on to act quickly.

At the next corner he glanced around. Yardley was advancing on the barn with his gun drawn; the moment he saw Nathan he jerked his gun up and fired. Splinters tore into Nathan's cheek, making him sway back and turn on his heel.

Gene was standing at the opposite corner of the barn. His posture was relaxed and confident, as it had been when he'd sneaked up on him on the rise.

His options of running either to the left or to the right being cut off, Nathan ran straight ahead, reckoning that Gene was enjoying his sport and wouldn't shoot him in the back.

This route took him past the side of the house. After running for ten paces, making a sudden decision he veered towards it.

He'd covered another five paces when two quick gunshots blasted out. They kicked dirt beside his feet, and when he looked over his shoulder he found that he'd moved far enough away from the barn for Yardley to see him.

Yardley must have fired low deliberately, so Nathan ran on. Another two shots rang out, both shots slicing into the ground a few inches ahead of his pounding feet, but they didn't deter him from running on.

On this side of the house the wall was only two feet high; he easily vaulted it and ducked down. Most of the back wall of the building had fallen down, allowing him to see the open plains stretching for miles ahead.

He had yet to see his pursuers' horses; he presumed they were in the barn, from which he was now cut off. His feeling of hopelessness growing, he moved on, doubled over, to the back of the house and looked around for cover.

His gaze alighted on a mound. It had a sloping top and he presumed that it might once have been a dug-out before the house and barn had been built.

Seeing no other choices, he ran to the mound and hunkered down at the side.

His pursuers weren't visible, but then

again neither was any place to which he could now run. He edged around the mound, desperately seeking an option.

When one presented itself it was an even worse course of action than having no options.

The dug-out had a bolted door. As the gunmen had yet to move into sight he drew the bolt and flung the door open. Someone was already inside and he jerked away while ducking, but then he registered who the someone was and he turned back.

'Sheriff Armstrong Beck?' Nathan murmured.

The former sheriff grunted behind his gag and Nathan hurried into the dug-out. When his eyes became accustomed to the gloom he could see that Armstrong was tied securely to a chair facing the door.

He and Armstrong exchanged long looks that acknowledged their dire predicament. Then Nathan closed the door behind him.

'What did Gene say?' Livingston asked when Emerson returned to the law office.

Emerson frowned as he walked over to the stove to pour himself a coffee.

'I couldn't find him,' he said. He nursed his mug against his chest and enjoyed the fumes. 'Nobody has seen him recently.'

'The same goes for Oscar, but hopefully they'll all turn up soon.'

Emerson nodded and went to his desk, avoiding catching Livingston's eye so that he wouldn't notice his discomfort. Livingston hadn't looked for Gene, but he had dealt with Oscar's body.

Now the vagaries of the current in the creek would determine whether the body would ever turn up again. If it did, Emerson hoped that the ravages of time would mask the identity and the manner of Oscar's death.

'Someone in Hickory Point will know what's going on,' Emerson observed, slurping his coffee. 'We'll get to the truth even if we have to work our way through them all.'

Livingston looked at him, frowning. 'I admire your enthusiasm, but I fear Jeff will be the only one we'll ever know for sure was there. If nobody talks I'm not sure he'll get convicted of killing his opponent.'

Emerson put the mug down and chose his next words carefully.

'In that case, perhaps we should start with the alternative assumption that Jeff's innocent.' Emerson noted Livingston's sceptical look, but he continued: 'When we first arrested him with Nathan he appeared to be a hapless fool. So perhaps our first impressions were right and he got caught up in something he couldn't control.'

Livingston leaned back in his chair to consider this suggestion.

'I can see we'll work well together in our new arrangement. You always tell me what you think, even when it's contrary to my view. I appreciate that.'

Even though his tone suggested he

wouldn't act on Emerson's view, a twinge of guilt at deceiving his friend made him go to the window.

It was late afternoon; the town was bustling and as he watched people go by he wondered how many more men he would have to kill before he could return to his old life.

He reckoned it would turn out to be everyone connected with the illegal games, both now and four years ago; the thought made him hunch his shoulders as he turned from the window.

'But you don't appreciate my view enough to release him?'

'No. Jeff's still the most likely culprit. He'd been in a fight and the other fighter was lying dead beside him.'

'Except I gather that the circumstances are the same as four years ago, and back then your father released the injured fighter.' Emerson sat on the edge of his desk. 'So maybe that's what we were supposed to see.'

'Maybe, but that fighter got killed, suggesting the obvious was obvious for a reason.' Livingston raised a hand as Emerson started to object. 'Either way, sitting around here won't solve nothing. I'll get back to Hickory Point and talk to the townsfolk.'

Emerson nodded. 'Doing anything is better than sitting around here waiting for something to happen.'

Emerson moved to rise, but Livingston bade him stay.

'You need to rest. You still look ill.'

Emerson hadn't been feigning his lingering nausea, so he had no need to put on a sickly expression.

'If you insist.' He tapped his chin. 'And I have an idea. I reckon nobody will talk, but they might heed a rumour.'

Livingston nodded. 'What rumour?'

'Tell them that Vencer Muerte is back.' Emerson smiled when Livingston furrowed his brow. 'It might make something happen.'

Giving a noncommital shrug Livingston took his departure, leaving Emerson to drink the last of his coffee and finalize the details of his risky plan.

The deputy shook his head. His recent problems had come about because he'd thought too much.

Years ago he had acted on instinct and had considered the consequences only later; acting in that manner again had improved his circumstances.

He put his coffee down unfinished and went to the small jailhouse. Their only prisoner was Jeff Morgan and, like the last time Emerson had checked on him, he was lying on his back, stiff and unmoving.

'Water,' Jeff murmured when Emerson approached the cell.

Emerson fetched a water bucket and rested the ladle against a bar, keeping it five feet from Jeff's grasp.

He wasn't being cruel. He reckoned that forcing Jeff to move would help him recuperate from his wounds more quickly than lying on his back, as that had been his experience when he himself had been on the receiving end of a beating.

Jeff responded by rolling off his cot

and crawling across the cell floor. He used the bars to raise himself, then stood hunched over, adopting the posture of a man twice his age.

'You look better than you did this morning,' Emerson said with a smile.

Jeff mustered a thin smile in response but it made his healing lips split open; he put a hand to his jaw and groaned.

'I feel as bad as I must look,' he said, hardly moving his jaw. He took the ladle and dribbled water into his mouth, although most of it ran down his chin to the floor.

'I've got some news that might soothe those bruises.' Emerson took the ladle and refilled it. 'You'll be freed tomorrow.'

Jeff's face brightened and this time he drank without spilling the water.

'When Sheriff Beck saw me earlier he didn't say nothing about that.'

Emerson winked. 'That's because he doesn't know you're leaving yet.'

17

'Gene Hansen's name keeps cropping up,' Livingston said when he arrived at the law office in the morning. 'He still hasn't returned to town so I reckon we need to look for him in Hickory Point.'

Emerson winced. He had anticipated some difficulty in persuading Livingston to leave town today while he himself remained in the office; this unexpected opportunity unsettled him.

'Sure,' he said. He rubbed his forehead and sighed wearily. 'But can we make the journey a slow one?'

'Is your head still hurting?'

Livingston gave him an odd look and when Emerson muttered that it did he came over to look at the back of his head, forcing Emerson to turn away so that the sheriff couldn't see that there was no injury.

'The lump's gone down, but I still

don't feel right,' Emerson said, probing around as if he were trying to find the exact spot.

'Then stay here. I need you fit for when this investigation heats up.' Livingston grasped Emerson's shoulders and manoeuvred him to a chair. Then he stood over him, waggling a warning finger. 'So if you don't feel better real soon, see Doc Taylor, and that's an order.'

Emerson said nothing other than to murmur his thanks, partly because he didn't want to risk continuing his act, but mainly because his friend's trusting response had made him feel guilty. While Livingston got ready to leave Emerson lowered his head.

When the office door had closed he paced the room, trying to work off his depressed mood. It didn't work, so he marched off to the jailhouse, determined now to do what he'd done yesterday and take control of the situation with decisive action.

Jeff was sitting up on his cot, his face

a mottled mass of bruises and cuts, but he looked back at the deputy with puffy eyes that were more animated than they had been yesterday.

'Have you had enough of sitting in there?' Emerson asked. He raised a key and dangled it between two fingers.

'Sure, but don't fill my head again with nonsense about leaving,' Jeff said.

'I wasn't lying.'

Emerson tossed the key towards the cell. It tinkled against a bar, which deflected its momentum so that it slid along the floor to stop beside Jeff's cot.

'The sheriff said nothing about freeing me.' Jeff looked down at the key. 'So what are you really after?'

Emerson folded his arms. 'It's looking bad for you. A dead man was found lying beside you. It looked like you defeated him in a bare-knuckle fight to the death.'

Jeff snorted and pointed at the various bruises on his battered person.

'I'm no fighter. In a fight to the death I'd die.'

'I know that. You couldn't defeat a formidable opponent. The trouble is, knowing the truth and proving the truth are two different things. If nobody's talking, the only option may be to find you guilty.'

Jeff leaned over the side of the cot and picked up the key. He sat up straight, wincing, then tossed the key in the air and caught it, this byplay clearly giving him time to think.

'I accept that, but the sheriff doesn't know you're here, does he?'

Emerson sighed. He had thought Jeff would be so eager to leave that he'd unlock the cell immediately.

'You're right to be suspicious,' he said, then added quickly when Jeff made as though to throw the key back to him, 'There's a catch. I want to use you to find the people who are really guilty.'

Jeff nodded several times, still clutching the key.

'That sounds dangerous.'

Emerson smiled now that he knew he had him.

'It is.'

Jeff got off the cot and stood up. 'In that case, who am I to argue?'

Without further discussion Jeff let himself out of the cell. He walked gingerly and groaned repeatedly, but Emerson stood back and let him make his own way.

Outside in the street nobody looked at them oddly. Jeff breathed in deeply as the fresh air hit him and he mustered a smile, but after he'd mounted up, he sat hunched over, wincing at his mount's every pace. They were well on their way out of town before Emerson spoke again.

'We're just going to ride along and see if your presence makes anything happen,' he said.

Jeff grunted with a pained grimace. He was riding stiffly in the saddle and was clearly suffering; Emerson was thankful that they wouldn't have to go far. He wasn't sure what he could try next if his hunch failed, as Jeff didn't look fit enough to trail around the county seeking out the men behind the fight.

As it turned out Gene Hansen was waiting at their first destination: an old oak three miles out of town; this was the place where, four years ago, Wardell Evans had met his untimely end.

'Is this the man you wanted to see?' Jeff said.

'Yeah,' Emerson replied.

'Why would he just happen to be waiting here?'

Emerson gave Jeff a long stare so that he'd realize the dark nature of his answer before he came out with it.

'Another boxer was once found dead here.' Emerson smiled as he saw Jeff flinch. 'But that was four years ago.'

This last comment appeared to reassure Jeff, although Emerson doubted he'd be so relaxed if he knew all the circumstances. The pair of them rode on.

'I didn't understand your message,' Gene called as they drew to a halt beside the tree. He cast a smirking glance at Jeff. 'But now that you're here I'm pleased you've decided to resolve matters this way.'

'I haven't come to hand over Jeff,' Emerson said. Gene narrowed his eyes. 'I came to broker a deal.'

'No deals, ever,' Gene snapped. 'You know that's how it works.' His hand twitched towards his holster.

Emerson spoke quickly to forestall any gunplay.

'Except I can offer the one thing your clients want to see: a bout between a previous Vencer Muerte and the current Vencer Muerte, to decide which man is the most worthy of the title.'

Jeff shot him a glance of dismay, then cast his gaze all about, presumably searching for a place to run to, having realized the sinister direction this conversation was taking. Emerson, however, was only interested in Gene's reactions.

On hearing the offer Gene frowned, his expression suggesting that he was interested but that his function was to serve his clients; they would make the important decision.

'As you've got yourself a death wish, come with me,' Gene said.

★ ★ ★

'When are we going to escape?' Nathan asked when the boredom of sitting in the dug-out at last overcame his relief at the postponement of his seemingly inevitable death.

'We do nothing until we get a clear chance,' Armstrong told him.

Nathan had been ready since first light and pangs of thirst, hunger and worry were all making him unsure about whether he could wait, but he bowed to the former sheriff's experience and settled down beside the door.

The previous night he had untied Armstrong's bonds within moments of finding him. Then, with Armstrong at his side, he had waited for Gene and Yardley to burst in, but they had only come as far as the door, where they had talked quietly.

Gene had snorted a laugh and had then bolted the door before leaving the dug-out. After that they'd been left alone; Nathan had suffered an uncomfortable night.

He'd explored the limited space and found that the underground section of the dug-out had fallen in, leaving just the one small room above ground where they now were. It was about ten feet square.

This morning he'd heard Gene move away and other riders arrive. The reason for these movements was unclear, but they only added to his uneasy feelings.

'What do you reckon Gene's got planned for us?' Nathan asked.

'I don't know.' Armstrong frowned. 'But he was waiting for someone.'

That answer gave Nathan no comfort and the pair sat in silence for a while before he spoke again.

'You do know I'm not involved with Gene, don't you?'

'I'd already worked out you'd just chosen the wrong way to make a quick dollar,' Armstrong replied. He glanced at the door. 'Will your accomplice help us?'

Nathan shook his head. Last night he'd detailed the events of the last few days, but he'd been too ashamed to mention that he'd left Jeff. Speaking in a low voice he now rectified that omission.

'There's not much hope in that tale,' Armstrong said when Nathan had finished. 'But don't worry. Even if Jeff can't come you can rely on my son to work out what's happening and find us. He's sure to be the next man to walk through that door.' He gave a reassuring smile, making Nathan relax for the first time since he'd entered the dug-out.

For the next hour they remained silent. Then, hearing the sound of bustling outside, Nathan edged closer to the door. Their only weapons were the ones they had improvised by breaking up the chair.

So Armstrong picked up a chair-leg in one hand and the rope that had been used to bind him in the other. Nathan contented himself with a double-handed grip of a chair-leg.

When they were in position on either side of the door Armstrong raised a hand, indicating that Nathan should wait for his order to act.

Outside, footfalls could be heard approaching the door, but they stopped a short distance away. Then hoofbeats sounded.

The riders drew up and a murmured conversation could be heard. Nathan caught Armstrong's eye and smiled, even though the speakers were too far away for him to hear what was being said.

'You were wrong,' Nathan whispered. 'Your son won't be the next man through the door. That's my friend Jeff.'

This news made Armstrong frown, but when a new speaker murmured something he brightened.

'Even better, one of the other men is my former deputy Emerson Tate,' he said.

18

Having stated his pitch Emerson stood before the line of three men. Jeff leaned on his shoulder.

Lone Gulch's three chief businessmen: Guy Atwood, Zack Snyder and Philip Winston, regarded him with cold eyes.

Emerson hadn't known that these days the fights were laid on for these men, but he'd met men like them four years previously and their stiff postures told him they were interested.

'I've heard you were once a good fighter,' Gene said.

'I still am,' Emerson said.

'Two nights ago these men paid to see a man fight. Why should they pay to see him kill you?'

'I've learnt plenty in the last four years. I'll wager my experience against his prowess.'

Gene's lips gave a knife-thin smile.

'And you hope he's still tired.'

Emerson spread his hands. 'Tactics like that come from experience.'

Gene acknowledged his point with a nod, then he turned to Philip, Zack and Guy. They all reached into their coat pockets and tossed bags to him.

'Two thousand dollars to the victor,' Gene said. 'Death to the loser.'

Emerson waited until Gene held the bags up before he replied.

'I agree to the terms, but not to the prize. I don't want money. I want you to let this man go free.' He pointed at Jeff, who was swaying as he struggled to remain upright after the long ride. 'He was set up to take the blame for the last fight but, unlike Wardell Evans, I want him to live.'

Gene snorted a laugh, suggesting he reckoned that negotiating terms was pointless when they were dealing with a man who wouldn't win.

'Agreed,' he said. 'If you win, he — '

'No. Whether I win or lose, he walks away.'

Gene narrowed his eyes. Emerson hoped he was more annoyed with the interruption than with his offer, and that he wouldn't consider its potential repercussions in too much detail. Gene still glanced at Philip, who nodded, before he replied.

'Agreed.' His harsh tone told Emerson his intervention was the last time he would accept being spoken to without respect. 'You'll fight the current Vencer Muerte, Drago. He killed his last opponent in ten minutes. I hope you last longer.'

Gene stepped back. The other three men turned on their heels and headed towards the barn. Jeff leaned towards Emerson.

'What you just did . . . ' he murmured, waving his hands as he struggled to voice his feelings.

'What I just did was repay a debt,' Emerson said.

'You owed me nothing.'

'I know.'

Jeff nodded, although Emerson doubted whether he knew that he was referring to Wardell Evans.

'You won't have a second, so how can I help?'

'Use this chance. After you leave never look back and never get involved with these people again.'

Jeff nodded and stood tall. Then, walking with difficulty, he walked beside Emerson as they made their way slowly to the barn. Gene and Yardley fell in behind them.

Emerson trudged along, conserving his strength and making no effort to limber up. He expected that the fight would get under way in the evening, but to his surprise when they entered the barn Drago was waiting for him.

His opponent was a head taller than Emerson. His shaven, misshapen head looked like a lump of granite and his massive fists looked as though they could grind granite into dust.

'The bigger they are . . . ' Jeff said, putting a hand on his shoulder.

'The harder they hit,' Emerson murmured.

'Nobody's guarding us,' Armstrong said. He had his ear pressed to the door.

Nathan gave a brief nod. After ten minutes of debate and bustle the last five minutes had been quiet. When he came to stand beside Armstrong at the door he could hear conversation and sounds of activity coming from the barn, though he couldn't tell what was happening.

'We've both got someone we can trust out there,' he said. 'I reckon we should help them.'

Armstrong nodded. He gestured to Nathan to stand back, then he stood side-on to the door. He made sure where the bolt was, then flexed his shoulder muscles as he prepared to run at the door. Before he could launch his move footfalls sounded outside. Then the bolt creaked as it was drawn back.

With no further exchange of words the two men positioned themselves to either side of the door, each standing in shadow. As the bolt scraped out of its hole, they raised their cudgels and advanced a pace.

Armstrong would see the incoming man first, so Nathan would let him make the first move; however, when the door creaked open for a fraction, Armstrong merely smiled and Nathan heard someone outside give a sigh of relief.

'I never expected to find you in here,' Livingston said.

'Come in, son,' Armstrong answered. He glanced at Nathan, indicating that he should lower his weapon. 'But who did you expect?'

The new sheriff of Lone Gulch slipped through the door. When he saw that Armstrong had company he smiled.

'Him,' he said, pointing at Nathan. 'I reckoned he was in league with Gene Hansen, but perhaps I got it wrong.'

'I'm sure that's the only thing you got wrong.' Armstrong patted his son's shoulder. 'I knew you'd figure out this situation better than I did and I'm looking forward to hearing how you did it, but we haven't got time to talk now.'

'We haven't, but you need to know one thing. Emerson Tate double-crossed us.'

'Emerson?' Armstrong spluttered. 'Are you sure?'

Livingston moved back to the door and opened it fully. He checked outside before beckoning them to join him. When Armstrong stood beside him in the doorway, he pointed at the barn.

'Emerson's over there. After the fight at Hickory Point he acted suspiciously. I gave him enough leeway to incriminate himself and he freed Jeff Morgan. Then he took him to the place where Wardell Evans was killed. He met Gene there and I followed them here. Now I'll end his activities.'

Armstrong snarled. 'Not if I get to him first.'

The two men looked at each other until Armstrong declined his head and edged backwards for a half-pace, acknowledging that his son was in charge. Then they slipped outside.

Feeling that he'd been forgotten, Nathan followed on behind. Outside they passed a man, presumably their guard, who was lying face down, unconscious.

The sight appeared to remind Livingston that he'd taken the man's gun; he withdrew it from his pocket and passed it to Armstrong. Emboldened, the former sheriff hurried to the side of the house, from where he peered around the corner at the barn.

The other two men followed and formed a line behind him, but when Armstrong turned to them he assumed an apologetic expression. Then he shuffled backwards to let Livingston take the lead.

Livingston shook his head and gestured for Armstrong to stay at the front.

'Take control,' he said. 'I don't mind.'

'But I do,' Armstrong said. 'I respect

the law. You take — '

'You two need to stop squabbling about who's leading this mission,' Nathan muttered, 'before it's too late to do anything.'

The two men glared at him until, to Nathan's amusement, they nodded simultaneously.

'My four years of being a lawman has taught me that when former prisoners talk sense,' Armstrong said, 'you know you're in trouble.'

All three men smiled. Then Livingston squeezed past his father to reach the corner, although he kept low so the other two men could look over his shoulder.

'We do what we did the last time,' he said. 'Everyone's in the barn and there's only one door, so we flank the door and go in fast. Except this time, anyone who doesn't throw down their gun doesn't live for long enough to get arrested.'

Armstrong nodded, but as neither man looked at Nathan he edged forward.

'And me?'

'Keep lookout,' the two men said together. Then they set off round the corner.

Nathan hated being left behind while Jeff's situation was uncertain, but he was armed only with a chair leg. He watched them keep low and move quickly, acting with the quiet efficiency of men who had worked together for years.

Armstrong took the nearside corner of the barn while Livingston scooted round to the back. Armstrong waited. Then, with uncanny timing, he moved on at the very moment that Livingston appeared at the other corner.

Walking sideways, they edged to the door. On reaching it Livingston glanced inside, then he drew quickly back and looked at Armstrong.

His expression was one of open-mouthed horror.

19

'And the harder they fall,' Emerson said to himself when for the fifth time Drago slammed down on to his back in a cloud of dust.

As Emerson paced around the fallen man, at the side of the barn Philip Winston was engaged in an animated conversation with the other two businessmen, Guy Atwood and Zack Snyder. This indicated more interest than he'd expected and it gave Emerson hope that he could complete the final part of his plan.

Yardley stood near to one side of the door while Gene guarded the other side. They frequently glanced outside while the third guard presumably still patrolled outside the dug-out.

He hoped that Gene and Yardley would relax and take themselves outside once the fight was over, giving him time alone with the watchers.

He intended to use that time to make them appreciate fully what it was like to fight to the death. But before he could do that he had to defeat his opponent, a task that was as unpalatable as it had been four years ago.

Drago had clearly won his previous fights using brute strength rather than fighting skill; now he was struggling against a man who did have that skill and who could move quickly.

The moment his opponent got to his feet Emerson darted in, his fists held before his face. As he'd done the last time, Drago lumbered forward with his arms outstretched, seeking to grab him in a bear hug.

Emerson ducked beneath the arms and thudded a quick blow into his stomach. It was like punching a wall and Emerson was pleased that he hadn't thrown his weight behind the blow; instead, he used his close position to kick the back of one of his opponent's knees.

Drago couldn't avoid going down on that knee, bringing his head below Emerson's eyeline. Emerson bunched his hands together and slammed a double-handed punch down on the back of Drago's neck.

Drago's neck muscles weren't as solid as those of his stomach and he tipped forwards to lie prone on the ground.

Emerson moved back quickly, not wanting to stay close to his opponent until he'd seriously weakened him.

Drago stayed down for thirty seconds, the same length of time as on the previous occasions he'd been toppled. Then, as before, Emerson moved in with his fists raised.

Again Drago lumbered forward, seeking to grab his opponent in a bear hug and again Emerson ducked under his arms. Then he hammered a quick punch that would further weaken his opponent, and kicked him over.

A follow-up punch, this time to his cheek, knocked Drago over on to his side; again Emerson moved away to await while the recovery process repeated itself.

Strangely, despite his early success, Emerson's confidence started to wane.

Drago had only one tactic, yet the last man he'd fought had looked as if he'd been crushed in a stampede. So, as that tactic clearly worked unless Drago tired, Emerson only had to make one mistake and Drago would then be able to grab hold of him.

Then, when Drago wrapped his massive arms around him, he'd squeeze the life out of him.

Emerson considered how he could weaken Drago more quickly, but before he could formulate a plan Drago got to his feet. So, continuing with his tactics, Emerson moved closer with his fists raised.

In response Drago stomped forward with his arms outstretched. His slack-mouthed expression made him look like a huge child taking his first steps.

Emerson moved to duck beneath his arms, but the comical image he'd conjured up distracted him. So he abandoned his planned punch-and-kick manoeuvre; instead he danced back on his heels.

He was pleased he'd acted in this way as, with alarming speed, Drago moved his arms down and closed them around the spot where Emerson would have been standing if he'd not stepped away.

Even more alarmingly, Drago's eyes glinted with malice before he resumed his usual bovine expression.

He lumbered forward. Emerson back-stepped away quickly as he tried to work out what had just happened. Drago had changed his seemingly sole tactic, and that implied the working of a keener intellect than he'd shown previously.

Drago must have picked up on his thinking, for he came to a halt and stood tall. He set his feet wide apart, bunched his fists and, grinning all the while, he aimed quick, strong punches to the right and left with the speed of a spooked rattler.

Then he offered Emerson a slow wink before he moved on, but this time he stepped lightly.

With a nod Emerson acknowledged that he'd underestimated his opponent and had nearly fallen into his cunning trap. Then he put on a worried expression as he laid the groundwork for his own play-acting. He shuffled backwards while looking around, as if he were seeking a place to hide.

Even if he had wanted to run, he'd have failed, for Gene and Yardley were at the door, watching the fight eagerly, presumably having known how Drago would act.

Philip Winston was edging forward in anticipation of a quick end. Only Jeff looked concerned, but he was eyeing Philip and the other businessmen with contempt, showing that Emerson would have an ally if he could defeat Drago.

Emerson reckoned his best hope was to stay out of Drago's reach for as long as possible and hope he got lucky. So he kept moving away, seeking to go in a wide circle, but Drago forestalled that move by darting sideways to cut him off.

Emerson doubled back and sought to go round Drago the other way. This time Drago let him pass, but that took Emerson into the corner of the stables.

With a smirk, Drago swung round and stomped to a halt in a position where with a single step he could grab him no matter in which direction he went. Then he took a long pace towards him.

Emerson decided not to wait until he'd been trapped; he ran to the left. Drago followed him with a sidestep, but Emerson had anticipated that move and, still looking to the left, he threw himself to the right.

Drago reacted quickly. His massive arm swung down to block Emerson's way. So Emerson flung himself to the ground. He skidded, rolled, and then, when he'd moved past his opponent, he came up running.

Ahead was the open barn door. To his surprise Armstrong and Livingston stepped into view. The unexpected sight made him stumble.

A moment later Drago's meaty hand slapped down on his trailing foot and tugged him backwards.

Emerson slammed down face first in the dirt. Drago reeled him in. Emerson kicked out, but he couldn't shake himself free of his captor's clutches.

With calm efficiency, Drago moved hand over hand until he had one hand on Emerson's thigh and the other on his hip. Then he twisted him over on to his back.

Emerson had a fleeting sight of the doorway where Armstrong and Livingston were raising their guns. He looked up into Drago's grinning face as Livingston's clear voice rang out:

'You're all under arrest,' he said. 'Do not resist.'

If Drago heard the command he didn't show it. He dropped down on to Emerson's chest, flattening him to the ground as if he were a bug squashed beneath a boot. While Drago was still off balance Emerson gathered his strength. With one frantic motion he tried to buck him.

Being winded he couldn't bring much force to bear, but he managed to make Drago slide off him and on to his side. Then he threw himself forward to wrap both hands round Drago's throat.

Unlike in his bout with Oscar yesterday, he couldn't wrap his hands entirely around his opponent's throat, but he did manage to clamp them beneath Drago's chin. He pressed in. Drago tried to roar, but the sound he emitted was reedy, giving Emerson hope that he'd closed off his windpipe.

Then Drago fought back. A flat-handed blow mashed Emerson's ear against the ground making his head ring like a bell, while a chop to his ribs made him think he'd been sliced in two.

Still he held on and, as he had done with Oscar, he unfocused his eyes and concentrated on his task.

Another chop slammed into his ribs. A crack sounded. He thought that Drago had broken a rib; then, through the buzzing in his ears he heard

Armstrong's voice ring out.

'Make sure Guy Atwood is the only one to die,' he shouted. 'Order the others to throw down their guns, Gene.'

Somebody shouted. Then rapid gunfire blasted out.

Emerson put these sounds from his mind and, as gunfire peppered away, he squeezed. He reckoned he was getting the upper hand as Drago flinched and didn't hit him again.

When he leaned back he saw a red patch spreading on Drago's side. He couldn't tell if the lawmen had shot him deliberately, but Drago's eyes had rolled back and his arms were dangling slackly.

More confident now, he glanced around the barn. Livingston and Armstrong were kneeling down beside the doors while, sprawled on the floor halfway down the barn was the body of stable owner Guy Atwood.

Gene had moved over to protect Philip and Zack. Yardley was running towards the lawmen, forcing Armstrong and Livingston to take him on. Yardley squeezed out a wild shot on the run before Armstrong shot him in the side.

Yardley ran on for two paces before he folded over and went to his knees. Then he looked up. He was facing two men with guns aimed at him.

As he struggled to raise his own gun two shots slammed into his chest. He keeled over.

Then the lawmen looked to the other end of the stables. Emerson followed their gaze to see the two survivors huddled behind Gene. He looked at their cowering forms with disgust; then he looked down at Drago.

The big man raised a hand for a few inches, then it flopped down to the ground. Reckoning he'd nearly defeated him, Emerson rolled over on to the barrel of Drago's chest and settled his weight upon it. Then he bore down.

Jeff, standing at the side of the barn, looked at him with horror. Emerson smiled reassuringly. Jeff only shuffled away towards Zack, who edged towards him with a gun drawn and held low.

Emerson could see the likely turn of events, in which Jeff would be taken hostage. He abandoned his attempt to finish off Drago. He leapt to his feet and broke into a run.

Jeff watched him, shaking his head, but when Emerson had covered half the distance towards him Jeff saw his intent. He swung round to face the real source of danger.

Zack advanced on Jeff with an arm outstretched, but he didn't reach him. With a shoulder down Emerson barged into Zack and carried him backwards until he slammed into the wall.

The air blasted from Zack's chest with a satisfying grunt. Before he could recover Emerson grabbed his gun arm.

Still disoriented, Zack struggled, but his gun became caught up in his jacket. This gave Emerson enough time to get a firm grip of his wrist and turn the gun.

A shot rang out, the sound booming in the cavernous barn. Then Zack's eyes glazed and he slid down the wall, leaving the gun in Emerson's hand.

Grinning widely at the successful outcome of his decision to fight back, Emerson moved away from the wall and swung round. He was facing Gene and Philip Winston, the latter being the sole survivor from the watchers.

Elsewhere in the barn the lawmen were shouting, but Emerson didn't concern himself with their plans. He took a long pace away from the wall and picked his first target. Philip stared with horror at the fallen man, then he looked at Emerson.

A solid punch hammered into Emerson's lower back, the force greater than that of any punch that had ever landed on him before. He was chiding himself for failing to finish Drago off when a second punch slammed high in his back.

He dropped to his knees.

He could see Philip looking at him but he appeared to be a great distance away; the orders ringing out in the barn also sounded as if they were being shouted in the distance.

Just as his slow reflexes told him he'd been shot the ground appeared to be coming up to meet him. He thudded face down into the dirt.

For the first time hitting the ground didn't hurt.

20

'Stay down, Jeff,' Armstrong shouted. 'We have this situation under control.'

Despite this order Jeff crawled to Emerson's still body and turned him over. Armstrong put him from his mind and turned his attention to Gene and Philip, who were both standing hunched over.

He glanced at Livingston to coordinate their movements. Then they headed into the barn, Livingston walking alongside one wall and Armstrong the other.

'You're four years too late,' Gene said.

'The law never forgets,' Armstrong said. 'Today we've ended your activities.'

'They've only just begun. You'll never stop everyone who shares our passion for the purest form of fighting.'

Armstrong didn't reply, accepting that his opponent was talking in the hope of distracting him. Seemingly proving this belief, Gene turned to Philip. This movement put his back to them so Livingston shouted at him to turn back.

A moment later Gene jerked round, a gun already in hand and aimed at Armstrong.

Gunmetal gleamed in Philip's hand too; his weapon was snapping up to aim at Livingston. Without a moment's thought Armstrong fired at Philip's chest before the man could shoot his son.

At the same moment another gunshot blasted. It didn't distract Armstrong and he fired a second time, this time at Philip's head. His target dropped to his knees and rolled over, face down.

Armstrong jerked his gun arm to one side to pick out Gene. But he stayed his fire when he saw the man stumble and go down on one knee; then he keeled over with blood spreading across his chest.

'Nice shooting, son,' he said.

'All those years spent working together paid off,' Livingston observed with a smile, and he hurried across the barn to the injured man.

Armstrong nodded, although in all their years of working together they'd never dispatched each other's opponents before. He checked on the other men as Livingston kicked Gene's gun away.

He could see that nobody had any fight left in them. He gestured at Jeff to leave the barn. This time Jeff did as ordered, although as he passed he shot him a surprisingly aggrieved glare.

Armstrong came to stand beside Livingston and the two men regarded the only survivor.

'Still got a passion for the fight?' Armstrong asked.

'Quit gloating, lawman,' Gene replied. He gritted his teeth and clutched his midriff.

'You're forgetting something. I'm not a lawman now. That means I'm free to do as I please, and I reckon you deserve the same treatment as Grant McClellan got.'

Livingston remained impassive and

Armstrong's self-assurance made Gene gulp and shuffle away towards the wall.

'Don't,' he murmured.

For several seconds Armstrong kept his gaze stern, then he lowered his gun.

'I could do it, but you've made me realize I still have a passion for the law.' He glanced at his son, who smiled. 'He's yours.'

'Or yours,' Livingston said. 'With Emerson's demise, I need a new deputy.'

Armstrong smiled and moved to take Gene's arm.

★　★　★

'I never thought we'd get out of this,' Nathan said when Jeff joined him.

'Neither did I,' Jeff said. He glanced over his shoulder at the barn. 'But I'm only alive because of Emerson Tate.'

'Emerson?' Nathan said, shaking his head. 'He was behind most of what's been going on here.'

Jeff stared at him with an incredulous

expression and turned on his heel to go back to the barn. Nathan followed him.

Inside, the only men still standing were Armstrong and Livingston. The only other survivor was the badly wounded Gene.

'Emerson saved my life,' Jeff said, facing Livingston.

'Then that was an accident,' Livingston said. 'Emerson double-crossed everyone. We may never piece together all of his crimes.'

'But he fought here knowing he'd probably . . . '

'You should also know that I've yet to prove you weren't involved,' Livingston said, glaring harshly at the man. 'Defending Emerson isn't a good way to convince me you're innocent.'

Jeff opened his mouth to continue arguing, but Nathan took the wise action of dragging him away. With the lawmen glaring at them they shuffled away until they were standing over Emerson's body.

'You believe me, don't you?' Jeff said,

turning to Nathan.

'If you say Emerson was our ally, then he was,' Nathan said.

Jeff knelt down beside the dead man. 'Then that'll be the only recognition he'll get for his bravery.'

Nathan nodded and knelt on the other side of the body. He glanced at the huge fighter whom Emerson had defeated, then laid a hand on Emerson's shoulder.

'The better they are . . . ' he said.

'The quieter they fall,' Jeff finished.

We do hope that you have enjoyed reading this large print book.

Did you know that all of our titles are available for purchase?

We publish a wide range of high quality large print books including:
**Romances, Mysteries, Classics
General Fiction
Non Fiction and Westerns**

Special interest titles available in large print are:
**The Little Oxford Dictionary
Music Book, Song Book
Hymn Book, Service Book**

Also available from us courtesy of Oxford University Press:
**Young Readers' Dictionary
(large print edition)
Young Readers' Thesaurus
(large print edition)**

For further information or a free brochure, please contact us at:
**Ulverscroft Large Print Books Ltd.,
The Green, Bradgate Road, Anstey,
Leicester, LE7 7FU, England.
Tel:** (00 44) **0116 236 4325
Fax:** (00 44) **0116 234 0205**

Other titles in the
Linford Western Library:

FROM THE VINEYARDS OF HELL

Harry Jay Thorn

When Texan and ex-lawman Captain Joshua Beaufort is captured by Union troops during the Civil War, he is given a choice — help to end the war on their terms, or spend the rest of it in a prisoner-of-war camp. Persuaded that it's in his best interests to cooperate, he rides in the company of young Corporal Benbow to his home state of Texas — back to old loves, old friends and old enemies. His task: to bring back the head of Buford Post, a notorious warmonger and gunslinger . . .

MARSHAL OF THE BARREN PLAINS

I. J. Parnham

When Marshal Rattigan Fletcher failed to stop Jasper Minx raiding the Ash Valley bank, he and his deputy Callan McBride were forced to leave in disgrace. In the town of Redemption, the pair are hired to find out why men from the Bleak Point silver mine have been disappearing — and when they discover that Jasper works there, they don't have to look far for a culprit. But as the miners side with Jasper, Rattigan will need all his instincts as a lawman if he is to bring his nemesis to justice . . .

REVENGE BURNS DEEP

Ethan Flagg

Army scout Green River Jim Claymaker's journey south is disrupted by a devastating prairie fire which claims the life of an old friend who has been scouting for a wagon train. The devious Ira Gemmel has his own reasons for preventing the wagon train from reaching New Mexico; so when he shoots the son of a Comanche chief, he puts the blame on Claymaker and the settlers. Claymaker's proficiency and courage are tested to the limit to bring the real perpetrator to justice and save the pioneers from the avenging Indians.

WAY OF THE LAWLESS

P. McCormac

Joe Peters and his partner Butch Shilton have been on the run for a year. On their way to prison for shooting a cheating gambler, a gang of outlaws murdered their escort — a crime for which the pair have been blamed. Trouble follows them everywhere, and they end up in the brutal Los Pecos penitentiary. Breaking out, they flee to Mexico, only to fall foul of the notorious bandit Barca. With enemies closing in on all sides, could this be the end of the trail for Butch and Joe?